Neumann

Kingdom of the Dwarfs

Text by Robb Walsh

Illustration and Concept by David Wenzel

Centaur books inc.
799 Broadway — New York, N.Y.

Centaur Books, Inc.
799 Broadway
New York, New York 10003

Table of Contents

To Janice

*Dr. Dvaergen discusses the dig in England with
Robb Walsh (left) and David Wenzel (right).*

Foreword

Throughout the world, stoneworks and monuments of an older human order have captivated the imagination of scholars. Monuments like Stonehenge, a perfect astronomical clock, and entire cities, such as those in the Indus Valley civilization, built thousands of years before the advent of modern man have created speculation that the rise of our savage forefathers arrested the development of a more advanced people.

Who were these ancient astronomers and city builders?

According to Dr. Egil Dvaergen, they were the ancient race of dwarfs. Dr. Dvaergen is a professor of anthropology and classical Norse literature at Storhamar University in Norway. Born with a congenital spinal defect, Dr. Dvaergen is himself a "dwarf." His affliction sparked an early interest in the dwarfs of legend and fable. In this ancient lore, Dvaergen found compelling evidence (substantiated later in his archaeological research) that a highly advanced, dwarf civilization prevailed on earth long before the emergence of man.

In the oral history of the Arayan invasion of India, our primitive ancestors describe the inhabitants of the Indus Valley City as "the monkey people" because of their small stature. Scholars exploring the stone ruins have often encountered folklore attributing these buildings to the dwarfs of some remote antiquity. Such was the case when Meadows Taylor examined the cromlechs of India in the early 1800's:

"Wherever I find them, the same tradition was attached to them, that they were the 'Morie humu,' or Morie's houses; these Mories having been the dwarfs who inhabited the country before the present race of men."

Dwarfs appear in Egyptian wall paintings, in Norse mythology, and in the legends of Europe. In every case they are connected with the making of fantastic metal works: In Egypt intricate copper artifacts; in Europe fabled treasures, gold rings, and magic swords. Dvaergen theorizes that the dwarfs continued living in the midst of our culture, practicing the technology of metallurgy, perceived by our ancestors as a power of magic.

Around the twelfth century, all mention of dwarfs in written literature suddenly ceases. According to Dvaergen, the spread of Christianity brought about the demise of the dwarf culture. Their metallurgy was considered magic, and in the eyes of the church, they were a heathen race of strange, little people. And so they were banished, while every trace of their heritage and achievements was effaced by the Christians.

Dvaergen's theories are well known and widely discussed in academic circles. Friends around the world advise him of new findings concerning ancient dwarfs. That is why I insisted Dr. Dvaergen be informed of my discoveries on the estate of Sir Rupert Grootes, discoveries that led to the excavation of the incredible ruin of Aegol Barrow.

Sir William Plum
Associate Director
Royal Academy of
Archaeological Sciences
London

The Discovery

Royal Academy archaeologists began their dig in the geranium beds where Sir Rupert Grootes uncovered a remarkable ancient dagger. In the first day of exploration, an axe-head was unearthed at a depth of four feet, at seven feet skeletal remains were discovered. Because of this evidence, Sir Rupert reluctantly allowed the archaeologists one year to explore on the grounds of his estate at Aegol Barrow near Durham in northern England. Sir William Plum, Associate Director, Royal Academy of Archaeological Sciences, London, headed the dig team.

**ROYAL ACADEMY OF
ARCHAEOLOGICAL SCIENCES**
Sir William Plum, *Associate Director*

May 11, 1979

Dr. Egil Dvaergen,

Your background as a scholar of antiquity and particularly your anthropological work on dwarfs impels me to apprize you of an exploration which I suggest will be of great interest to you.

In April of 1979, a curiously marked dagger discovered in northern England was examined by our academy. The blade metal of this artifact was identified as tempered steel. Carbon dating placed its age at no less than 1500 years, indicating its manufacture preceded the iron age by 500 years.

The dagger was discovered by Sir Rupert Grootes, noted botanist, on his estate at Aegol Barrow while Sir Rupert was enlarging his geranium beds. He reluctantly allowed us to begin an excavation in his newly planted flower garden.

At a depth of 7 feet skeletal remains were discovered. My associates concluded that the bones represented two skeletons interred together, one a grown man, the other a child. This conclusion was drawn from the disproportionate size of a large skull to some smaller rib fragments. The bones lay in front of a smooth stone wall bearing a runic inscription.

My associates filed a report concluding that the site was a Viking grave. Indeed, the runic inscription was Scandinavian, and not nearly as old as the weapons. They credited the Vikings penchant for collecting exotic weaponry as the source of the ancient dagger and axe.

The matter is considered closed here, but my conscience as a scholar directs me to inform you of my opinion that something much more remarkable than a Viking grave lies below Sir Rupert's geranium patch at Aegol Barrow. I am convinced that the inscription marks the entrance to a subterranean chamber. The skeletal remains thought by the students to be that of a man and a child are actually the bones of a single dwarf.

I have notified the Academy that you have been invited as an expert in Scandinavian antiquity to examine the site. I invite you to explore the find under the conditions I must here make clear.

The academy is publicly funded to study Britain's past. We must avoid controversy to retain our endowment. We cannot, therefore, be connected with an excavation as speculative and potentially controversial as this one. We have the permission of Sir Rupert to explore the premises until the spring of next year when he must replant his beloved flowers. Until that time you are free to examine any and all artifacts and ruins located on his property. British law dictates that artifacts found in Britain are the property of the state and its people. You may not therefore remove any artifacts from the site as the Academy is in no position to present them to the Royal Museum. Please keep this matter confidential for now.

Within these bounds I wish you the best of luck and encourage you to keep in touch.

Sincerely,

Sir William Plum

Sir William Plum discovers an inscription while his researchers examine an unusual skeleton. Because of the controversial nature of Sir William's findings, the Academy elected to close the dig. The Royal Academy's embarassing involvement in the "Piltdown Man" scandal has made them particularly sensitive to controversy. Sir William agreed to cease his exploration on the condition that he be allowed to invite Dr. Egil Dvaergen, an anthropologist specializing in the study of ancient dwarfs, to continue the exploration.

The Door to Aegol

We stood assembled before the entranceway Sir William's crew had unearthed. In two short weeks we had collected an impressive group of experts. Dr. Lars Wein of Sweden, a noted metallurgist, stood fondling the axehead the archaeologists had discovered here. Dr. John Scott, an English folklore expert, conferred with Robb Walsh, a student of ancient literature, on the inscription above the doors. The language was Old Norse, the legend read "Kingdom of the Dwarfs." David Wenzel, an illustrator, sat on the bank of earth sketching the scene and I, Dr. Egil Dvaergen, concerned myself with the efforts to budge the stone doors.

With hammers and chisels we had chipped away the hardened mud which sealed the entrance. We had tried prying with crowbars, and digging under the doors with no success. While the exhausted and impatient team rested, I began tapping with a small hammer, sounding the doors, listening for weaknesses in the rock. A rumble went up as I hit along the top crack, and the doors suddenly began to swing open of their own weight.

The party rushed forward, everyone struggling for a handhold, guiding the doors further and further apart. Our entrance was at last assured. We stood silently for a moment peering into the darkness, listening to the thunderous echo of the opening doors resounding in the chambers below, smelling the ancient musty odors that rose with the dust.

I walked into the shaft, but turned to find my colleagues stooping or crawling. I realized then that the shaft was only four feet eight inches high. Ten feet into the opening, we were stopped by a wall, but a marvelous stone stairway curved down into the darkness. We decided to spend the afternoon in preparation for our first descent the next morning. By nightfall, our equipment was assembled. Spirits were high as we discussed our theories and expectations late into the night.

Early the next morning we made our descent. The tight winding stairway was obviously not designed for men of normal size. The small proportions led us to expect a claustrophobic series of chambers in the darkness below. We were dumfounded to discover a hall the size of a London train station at the bottom of the stairs. Carved stone columns more than forty feet in height stood in rows as far as our flashlights enabled us to see.

Our first task was to confirm our suspicions about the inhabitants of this amazing ruin. Within an hour we had collected an assortment of ancient artifacts. Small hammerheads and miniature chisels, a sewing needle no more than half an inch in length and portions of a child-size coat of armor in various states of rusted ruin convinced us that Aegol Barrow was once the site of an underground dwarf civilization.

The overview of the first day's exploration revealed a central core of four levels. On the first level, the enormous Common Hall and the Throne Room of the dwarf king, one floor below, stood the foundry, and forges of metal smiths. The third level down was occupied by smelting furnaces, and the lowest level was a depot for a system of mining tunnels which ran for countless miles in all directions.

For the next eight months we explored this astounding underground ruin. Because of the deadline imposed by Sir Rupert Grootes, we gave up any plans of a full scale archaeological undertaking. We concentrated instead on the fascinating details of the dwarfs' underground existence. We have attempted to reconstruct through illustration portions of the kingdom as they once existed. From the dwellings and workplaces and artifacts we have tried to capture the likeness and spirit of the dwarfs who lived here.

Scholars will debate the findings of Aegol for years to come. Careful study will confirm or deny many of the theories and speculations we have set forth. We are convinced, however; after these months of exploration, that the dwarfs of Aegol are a lost race whose buried secrets hold the key to understanding the beginnings of technology and civilization on this planet.

warfs are a part of our dim recollections of the distant past. Ancient legends and folklore from all over the world describe dwarfs as hoarders of gold, builders of swords, and masters of alchemy. Christianity denounced the legacy of the dwarfs as part of pagan mythology and much of the truth about them was lost or forgotten. Scholars attempting to reconstruct the history of ancient times have come to the conclusion that dwarfs were, in fact, a technologically advanced race that preceded our own.

Life in the Underground

Armies of dwarfs armed with picks and shovels, sledge hammers and wedges attacked the mountain, slowly capturing her rich treasure of ore. The mines grew and slowly one cavern was abandoned as the dwarfs began to work the next. Over the years, the dwarfs became accustomed to the winding tunnels and the musty dark caverns. They discovered that their enemies feared the underground and would not follow them into the mines. They began to

store their valuables there. Under prolonged attack they moved entire villages into the abandoned caverns. Thus began the underground civilization of the dwarfs. Their adaptation is an incredible testament to their in-genuity. In their underground isolation they developed a flourishing culture and a technology hundreds of years ahead of anything on the surface.

Woodcutters

There were many supplies essential to the dwarfs which had to come from above. Along with food, the most important of these was timber. After their acclimation to the underground, the dwarf woodcutters became adept at cutting wood at night in forest clearings. They worked with torches and by moonlight, sliding the logs down into the tunnel openings. Their nocturnal working habits also aided in keeping the dwarfs out of their enemies' view.

Smiths of the Underworld

In the constant darkness underground, the dwarfs began to lose the distinction of day and night. Except for woodcutters and others with business above ground, the time of day was no longer important. This adjustment aided in the efficiency of the dwarf kingdom. The blast furnaces where iron was smelted must have worked continuously for months at a time. The intense fire of the furnaces and forges probably burned constantly, stoked by each new shift of workers.

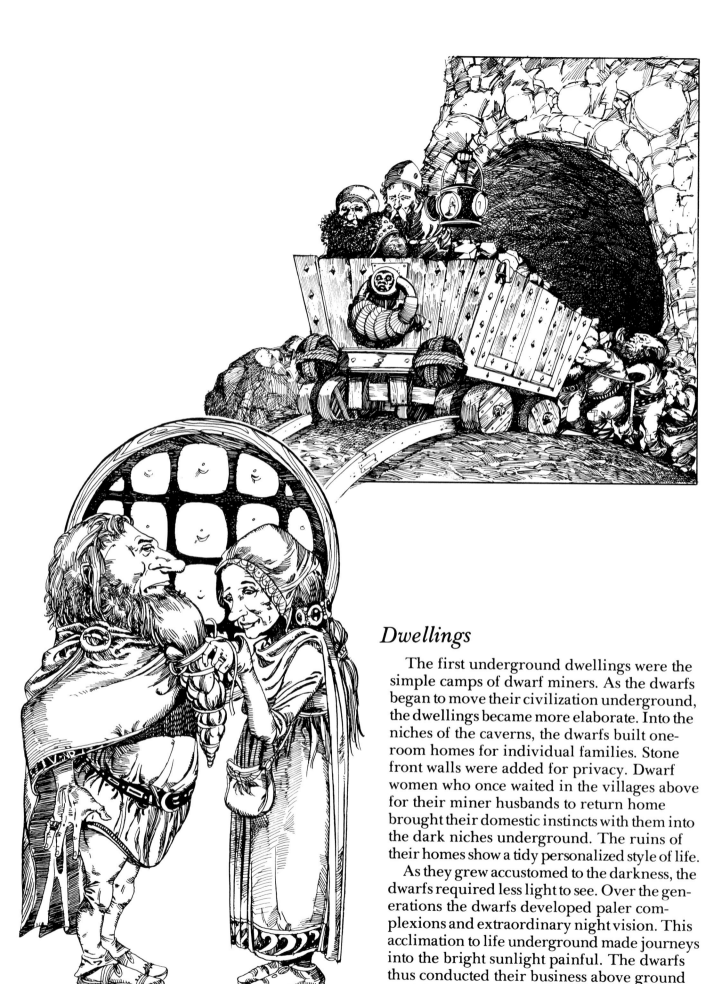

Dwellings

The first underground dwellings were the simple camps of dwarf miners. As the dwarfs began to move their civilization underground, the dwellings became more elaborate. Into the niches of the caverns, the dwarfs built one-room homes for individual families. Stone front walls were added for privacy. Dwarf women who once waited in the villages above for their miner husbands to return home brought their domestic instincts with them into the dark niches underground. The ruins of their homes show a tidy personalized style of life.

As they grew accustomed to the darkness, the dwarfs required less light to see. Over the generations the dwarfs developed paler complexions and extraordinary night vision. This acclimation to life underground made journeys into the bright sunlight painful. The dwarfs thus conducted their business above ground at night.

Crows

Perches and rookeries throughout the Kingdom testify to the dwarfs' fascination with crows.
The dwarfs trained these birds to mimic
human speech and they became the favorite
pets of Aegol. The Royal Wing had extensive
roosts and cages for the trained birds. In the
Common Hall, a booth was found where crows
were bought and sold.

Underground Fountain

Several streams and spring-fed brooks were diverted from above through aqueducts and culverts into the underground kingdom. The streams powered hammers in the forges and bellows in the furnace rooms. Water cooling was also required for the continuous operation of the blast furnace. Spring-fed brooks provided Aegol with drinking water which was drawn from communal fountains. While the dwarf men loitered in their free time around the Common Hall where conversation, mead and commerce flowed, the dwarf women lingered about the communal fountains.

29

The Common Hall

The Common Hall was the noisy hub of
activity in the dwarf kingdom. Its huge stone
expanse echoed the din of commerce; wooden
carts rolling over the stone floors, the bleats and
hooffalls of sheep being traded for metal farm
equipment, the cries of hawkers selling mead
by the draught or barrel, the shrill scream of
trained crows, the prized pets of the dwarfs, and
the laughter, conversation and arguments of
the dwarfs themselves.

The great stone columns at the Common Hall
are the oldest stone carvings found in Aegol,
their capitals are reminiscent of Egyptian
designs. Along with its daily use as a market
bazaar, the Common Hall functioned as the
scene of Aegol's great public celebrations.

In the Court of the Kings

A Royal Celebration

A feasting room in one wing of the Royal Hall was the scene of Aegol's private celebrations. The most beautiful maidens of Aegol waited on the King, his ministers and guests.

Mead was the beverage of celebration. Elaborate drinking mugs hung on the walls were brought down for royal toasts. Swords, shields and axes made famous in battle were displayed.

reasure of the Dwarfs

The Royal Hall

From the Royal Hall the throne of the dwarf kings commanded the center focus of the Kingdom. Two features about the Royal Hall are especially striking: its opulence, and its security system. The security system included a series of iron grates which could be lowered to cut off the Royal Wing from the rest of the Kingdom. The opulence of the throneroom created a showcase to display the treasure of the dwarf kings. The majesty of the king was symbolized by his treasure. For the dwarfs, treasure seemed to have a power beyond wealth.

From the well-preserved ruins of the halls of Aegol we were easily able to visualize the kingdom as it once existed. A comparison of the Royal Hall ruin sketched above with the reconstruction on the facing page illustrates the faithful technique of Aegol's recreation.

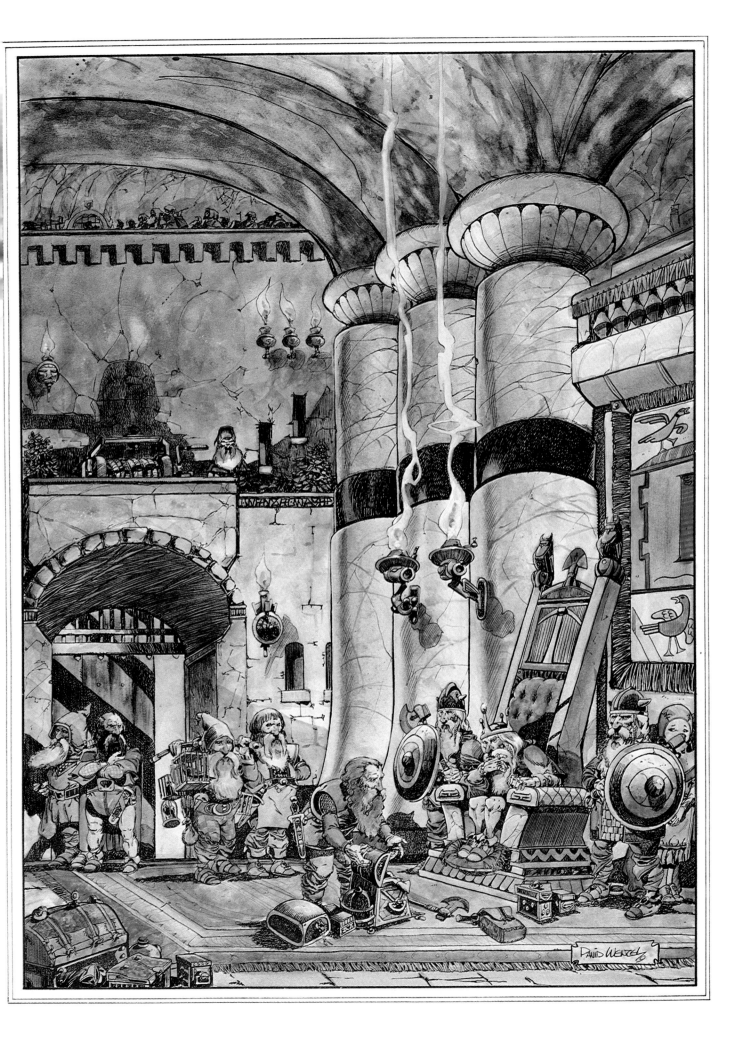

Dwarf King and his Treasure

The power of the dwarf king was embodied in his treasure. Dwarfs hoarded treasure, their collections of precious metals and richly ornamented weapons were fabled and envied. Treasure was not used for buying or bartering or backing currency. For the dwarfs, treasure was an end in itself. The dwarfs didn't steal treasure or buy it or obtain it in the ways of men. They wrested it from the earth herself. This was the power that treasure symbolized, mastery over the earth and her riches.

Goldsmiths

The dwarfs' incredible skill with stone and metal crafting, scholars of antiquity suggest, was a result of their physiology. The smaller hands and tools of the dwarfs gave them an incredible dexterity. This natural advantage led them to found their culture and their ideal of achievement on the manipulation of natural elements. This ideal expressed itself in stonework, architecture, technology, and in exquisite handiwork of golden treasures.

Nowhere was the dwarf ideal better personified than in the dwarf goldsmiths. The goldsmiths must have been the most highly regarded artists in the kingdom for they were the creators of its treasure.

Dwarf goldsmiths were the inheritors of a long tradition of excellence; their techniques had been refined over the course of centuries. The layout of the gold smithy at Aegol suggests a system of guilds each specializing in a particular aspect of gold working. Each guild had a master, several smiths, and apprentices who dedicated their lifetimes to the perfection of one area of goldsmithing.

Mining and Metalworking

Foundry

White hot iron is poured in the foundry. Large castings required ladles of molten iron to be transported quickly and poured at a precise temperature. Dwarfs who worked with hot metals were probably the victims of repeated burns and singes. The wizened and wrinkled appearance attributed to dwarfs was often a result of this constant exposure to flying sparks, intense heat, smoke and soot. Small water vats discovered in the metal working sections were probably used to soak clothing and beards to prevent scorching and to douse burns. These were the only safety precautions available.

The Bow Drill

With hammers, tongs and charcoal heat, the dwarf smiths performed their alchemy on iron. Absorbing carbon from the charcoal fire, iron was hammered and layered and heated again, forming highly carbonized steel. This fine steel was used in the bit of the dwarfs' bow drill, the first improvement over pick and shovel mining. The steel bit was inserted into fissures in the rockface. Bowmen spun the drill until the crack grew and the ore fell away. The drill was then forced further in and the process repeated.

The Water Pump

Rusted elements of a simple pump were discovered in the deepest levels of the dig. The apparatus was mounted on a boat or raft and powered by two dwarfs working a see-saw configuration. Hoses were probably made of wrapped hides. The pump enabled the dwarfs to control flooding, but more importantly, the principle it employed led to the discovery of steam power.

Serpent-Headed Pile Driver

The most colossal achievement of the dwarf mining technology was a steam-powered pile driver. The equipment utilized the chamber and piston principle invented for the pump to propel a carburized-steel battering head with astonishing velocity. Huge mechanical shovels scooped up the broken rock.

The pile driver and mechanical shovels were decorated with fascinating details. The pile driver was fashioned to represent a giant serpent. Eyes and facial features were cast in the steel battering head. The mechanical shovel resembled a dragon. Perhaps intended as an homage to mythical creatures, these fearsome likenesses were certainly used as a means of frightening off intruders. Many of the mine shafts surfaced into the countryside, so one can only surmise how the countless tales of fire-breathing dragons evolved from the steam-breathing pile drivers and mechanical shovel.

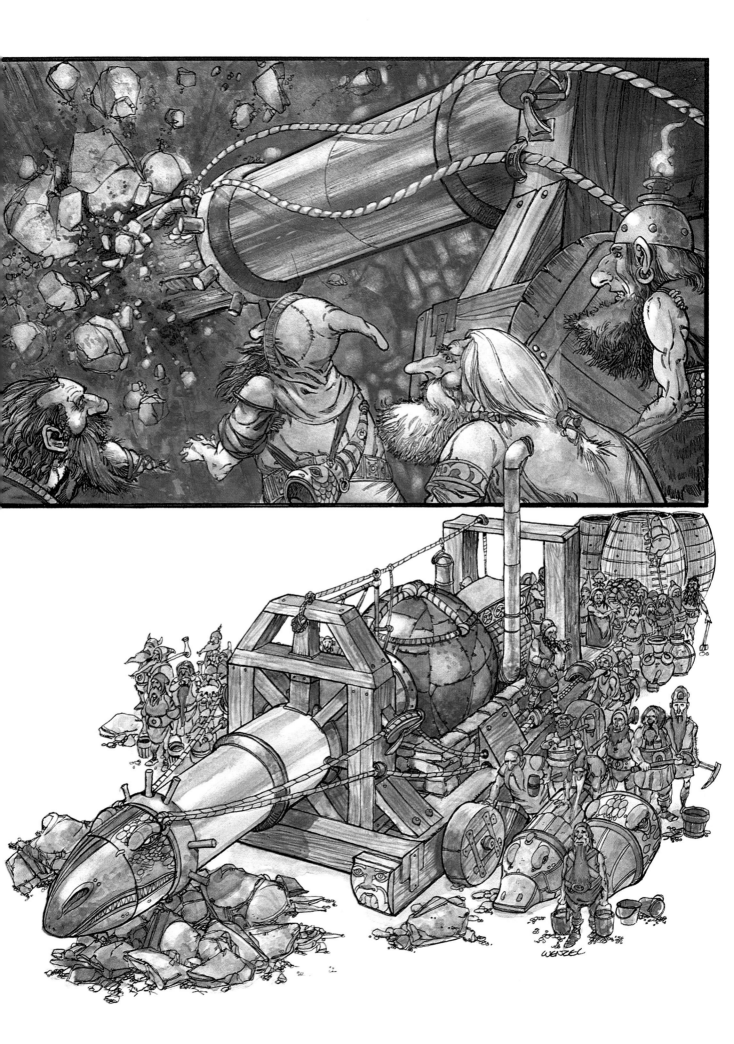

Medieval Sorcery:
The Blast Furnace of Aegol

The smelting of high quality iron was the secret of the dwarf's metalmaking prowess. The most awesome sight in the underground kingdom must have been the massive blast furnace in full operation. It stood in the center of the cavernous third level of the kingdom, directly above the mining depot and below the foundry and forges.

The huge stone stack was connected to ten charcoal stoves which were in turn linked to an ingenious system of water-powered bellows. Despite their lack of coal or air turbines, the dwarfs managed to achieve the temperature of 2800 degrees Fahrenheit required to melt iron. The furnace probably required months to reach this temperature. Once the smelting began, it must have continued non-stop until the system broke down.

The process was as follows: high grade charcoal was heated in the stoves fanned by the water-powered bellows. Charcoal, iron ore, and a flux of limestone and slag were layered in the giant stack. When the temperature of 2800 degrees was reached, the iron melted, trickling through the charcoal which kept the temperature constant and gave the iron more carbon content. The flux attracted impurities. The stream of water which powered the bellows flowed through a space in the wall of the stack to keep the stone from crumbling. The enormous upward draft was partially vented back to the stoves, the rest of the exhaust was allowed to escape through a chimney to the outside. Hoppers near the top of the stack allowed more ore, flux, and charcoal to be added as needed. The molten iron flowed out of the base of the stack, the lighter slag was diverted and the pure iron flowed into sand molds on the floor or ladles which were winched to the foundry above to be poured into special casts.

This advanced metallurgical technology was not developed on the surface until the 1400's. Carbon dating tests performed on the iron found in the dwarfs' blast furnace shows the last batch of iron was produced in Aegol around 1100 A.D.

Swords of Magic

Dwarf-made swords were reputed to have magic powers. In the legends of ancient Germany and Scandinavia, dwarfs were captured and held by the chiefs of the tribes for a ransom, often consisting of a magic sword. According to these legends, the outcome of a battle or the fate of a dynasty could hinge on the magic of a dwarf-made sword.

The dwarfs themselves characterized their swords with unique personalities. Swords were given names and specific purposes of missions. In the Weylund story, the saga of the last dwarf king, Weylund names his sword *Gram* and consecrates it to a mission of vengeance. In the story, *Gram* takes on a life of its own. Weylund is unable to stop the sword from completing the mission he has ordained.

The magic swords of the dwarf smiths derived their powers from meticulous handcrafting and strict testing. From before the time of Christ through perhaps the seventh century, the dwarfs manufactured the only steel weapons in Europe. The sorcery which produced magic swords was the laborious process of carburization. The dwarfs' carefully guarded secrets of steel-making were probably not fully understood by the dwarfs themselves. They may have regarded the process as magical, but they understood it was a sorcery that required hard labor, careful attention to detail and hours of sweat.

The dwarf sword-making process started with highgrade iron bars produced in the excellent blast furnaces of Aegol. Several bars were immersed in red hot charcoal in the smithy. The bars absorbed carbon from the coals, carburizing the outside of the iron bar into steel. The red hot bars were then hammered together creating a steel and iron sandwich. This construction gave the sword a steel edge for sharpness and layers of softer iron for flexibility. The shaft was then tempered and tested exhaustively before it was approved for use.

Testing the Temper

Testing the carburized sword shafts meant
smashing them against the anvil and watching
for bends or breaks. Broken shafts were melted
down again, and bent shafts were returned for
another tempering. The ideal sword shaft was
tempered enough not to bend, flexible enough
not to break. The only way to achieve this perfect
balance was through trial and error. Once
the shaft had passed this testing it was "tuned"
by the smith. Tuning involved filing and cutting
grooves to achieve an ideal weight and center
of gravity. The perfectly tuned sword had a
distinctive ring when struck.

At last the sword was meticulously sharpened, fitted with a handle and inscribed with
decoration of runic legends often including the
name or symbol of the smith, the date and
place of manufacture.

Singing Swords

The bell-like ring of a perfectly "tuned" sword was an important element of its magic. The sound of a good sword had a special power on the battlefield. Thus, the dwarfs paid special attention to a sword's "song," eventually discovering a unique tuning process which produced the singing swords of legendary fame.

Tuning meant filing a channel indentation into the middle of the shaft known as a blood groove. The groove allowed the sword to pass swiftly through flesh. Removing metal to form the groove also allowed the smith to adjust the weight of the sword until it rang with the desired resonance. To lighten larger swords, the dwarfs experimented with cutting a series of holes through the shaft. This resulted in a sword that hummed when passed quickly through the air. By adjusting the size and position of the holes, the hum could be harmonically adjusted to complement the ring made when the sword was struck. And so the sword that sang in battle was invented. Singing swords took on a magic animation, the music inspiring the wielder and terrifying his opponents.

Axes and Weaponry

While legends have made the swords of Aegol famous, they have tended to ignore the rest of the dwarfs' impressive arsenal. Master smiths gave equal attention to the making of spears and battle axes. The battle axe was the favored weapon of the Vikings and the dwarfs fashioned these awesome weapons in incredible variety. Iron shields, helmets and armor were meticulously custom designed for use by the warriors that Aegol armed.

warfs and Folklore

Dwarfs of Folklore

After the Norman Conquest, Britain was converted to Christianity. Christian persecution eventually brought about the demise of the dwarfs and the disappearance of all their knowledge and history. In their efforts to drive out heathen beliefs, the Christians erased much of Britain's past. Accounts of heathen times including the stories of the dwarfs were omitted and popular heathen figures like King Arthur were conveniently converted to Christianity in the rewritten version of Britain's history.

The experience and memories of the people who inhabited Britain before Christianity survived through the oral tradition of folklore, gaining embellishment and variation through generations of retelling. Thus, our memories of the dwarfs are preserved in the clouded and fantastic forms of folktales and children's stories. For this reason we have come to consider dwarfs in the same light as spirits, fairies, and creatures of make-believe.

Enchanted Forests

English fairy tales describe little people living underground in fairy mounds who surface by night to dance around their fairy fires in secret forest clearings. This description fits the working habits of the dwarf woodcutters with an accuracy that seems more than coincidental.

Acclimated to the darkness of the underground, the dwarfs were comfortable in the blackness of the nighttime forest. Cutting their supplies of timber in hidden clearings, the dwarf woodcutters worked throughout the night. Their campfires and torchlights glowed eerily in the mist of the damp forest. To the passer-by, this scene must have taken on an ominous and supernatural significance.

The dwarfs were probably responsible for many different kinds of English folktales. Along with the superstitious interpretations of chance sightings, are the tales of trolls and goblins which resulted from the dwarfs' tactics of frightening away intruders.

Little People of the Forest

Dressed in camouflage, a dwarf lookout watches for intruders while the dwarf woodcutters go about their nightly work. The passer-by who decided to investigate the campfires in the forest would have met the look-out at close range. After a piercing warning scream, the look-out and the woodcutters would retreat into the hidden openings that led back into the tunnels of Aegol.

The explanation of these events was left to the passer-by's imagination.

Secret Entrances

Secret entranceways gave the Kingdom of Aegol easy access to the world above. Their ingenious designs made them undetectable to anyone unfamiliar with their existence. The entranceways seemed to give the dwarfs the power to appear and disappear at will. While the system was intended as a defense to keep Aegol's whereabouts a secret, the dwarfs were not above using their advantage for an occasional act of mischief. Popping out of a tree stump and grabbing a sheep while the shepherd's back was turned was a favorite sport among the younger dwarfs.

Trolls

The human imagination was the dwarf's most powerful defense. By haunting the forests and roadsides in fantastic costumes, the dwarfs kept strangers away from Aegol. With mud and berry juice smeared on their faces, twigs and slime wrapped in their beards, and antlers, horns, and animal parts fastened to their heads the dwarfs challenged those who sought to invade the kingdom. Folktales regarding trolls, goblins, and black dwarfs were probably spawned as a result.

The dwarfs' method of protecting themselves gave the area a rich tradition of folklore, but in the end it backfired. The enchanted forests of Aegol gained such a reputation as the dwelling place of supernatural creatures that the Christian church made special efforts to cleanse the unclean spirits. Persecution of the dwarfs by the churchmen because of their magic powers and supernatural connections lead to the downfall of Aegol.

Dwarfs: the Ancient Terrorists

A tapestry discovered in the feasting room of the Royal Hall provides an excellent illustration of the dwarf's use of superstition and terrorism as a defensive weapon.

The tapestry tells the story of a group of Roman soldiers patrolling the forests of Aegol during the Roman occupation of Britain in the reign of Claudius. As the Romans advanced on the underground kingdom, the dwarfs were pressed to repel the invaders. A frontal assault against the Roman patrol would only have brought more soldiers down on Aegol, so the dwarfs launched a more ingenious kind of attack. Carefully making themselves up in the horrifying disguise of ferocious trolls and half-beasts, they burst out of the secret openings of Aegol at nightfall and ran at the Roman patrol. The horrified soldiers retreated to their fortress. They related the story of their ambush to the rest of their number and the forests around Aegol were never again patrolled.

Though fearless in battle, Roman foot-soldiers were extremely superstitious. The first invasion of England was flawed by a near mutiny because of Britain's reputation for supernatural occurences.

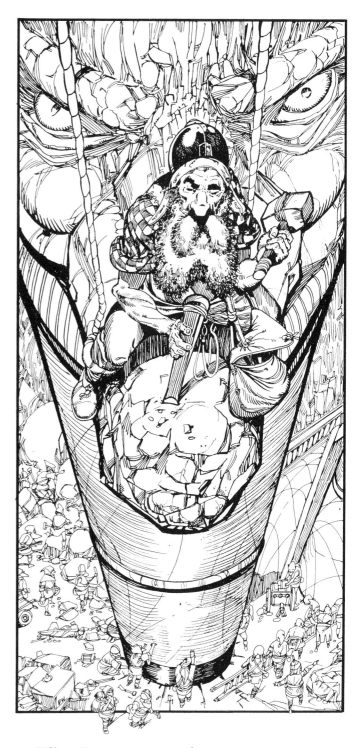

The Stone Dwarf

As legend has it, a dwarf would turn to stone
if he were exposed to sunlight. This legend
probably has its roots in the dwarf's masterful
stone carvings. A statue sculpted by the dwarfs
would no doubt be perceived by the village folk
as an enchanted dwarf turned to stone. The
dwarfs' avoidance of daylight was a result
of acclimation to the darkness of the underground.

Dragons

Among the discoveries made in the mine
shafts of Aegol was a steam pile driver, fashioned
to resemble a giant serpent. Close by it —
decorated to resemble a fearsome dragon —
was a mechanical shovel that had been used to
scoop up broken rock. The designs that em-
bellished this equipment were more than decoration. Several of the mine shafts and lumber
tunnels of Aegol opened into the countryside
and were too large to disguise. The mechanical
shovel seems to have doubled as a dragon-
sentry. Poised in the mouth of the tunnel, its
nostrils flaring like torches, this fearful appari-
tion stood ready to frighten away intruders.

Suddenly the tale of the brave knight who
ventured into the cave of the dragon and
emerged with dwarf gold gains plausability.
The dwarfs' mechanical shovel was no doubt
responsible for many of the dragon and monster
stories of the region, but the dwarfs' fascination
with dragons seems to have deeper roots. The
use of dragons in artwork and metal design
hints of some unknown reverence lost in
the dwarfs' own pre-history.

Writings of the Dwarfs

he Skald

Beowulf, The Lay of the Niblung, the Norse mythology, and all of the ancient legends of Northern Europe's oral tradition were first recorded by the skalds of Iceland, the inventors of written narrative. The Kings of Scandinavia enlisted the skalds as court poets to record the histories of their kingdoms and the exploits of their warriors.

We were astonished to discover in a secluded room below the Royal Hall that one such skald had inhabited the Kingdom of Aegol — probably a shipwreck victim. The sailing route from lower Sweden to Denmark passed the rocky coast of Aegol on the way to Iceland. The room designed for his use was built to normal human proportions; the only such room in Aegol. It was dominated by a huge writing desk and a collection of scrolls.

The writings begin with an account of the Golden Age, the period when dwarfs ruled the earth before the time of man. The details and descriptions of this epoch are vague and cryptic. Years of deciphering may be required before these chapters can be offered in translation. They are followed by biographies of the dwarf kings and princes.

We have translated in abridged form the biographies of the early dwarf kings to trace the history of Aegol. The story of Weylund, last King of Aegol, is offered in its entirety. It is the most complete account of a dwarf-hero and provides us with an interesting glimpse of Aegol at its height. The Turold story comes from the cycle of dwarf princes who ruled Aegol after Arthur. It includes an account of the Norman invasion which led to the downfall of Aegol. The skald appears to have been present into those last dark days of the kingdom. By whatever accident he came, we are grateful that he stayed to record the oral history of the dwarfs. It is a history that otherwise might have perished with them.

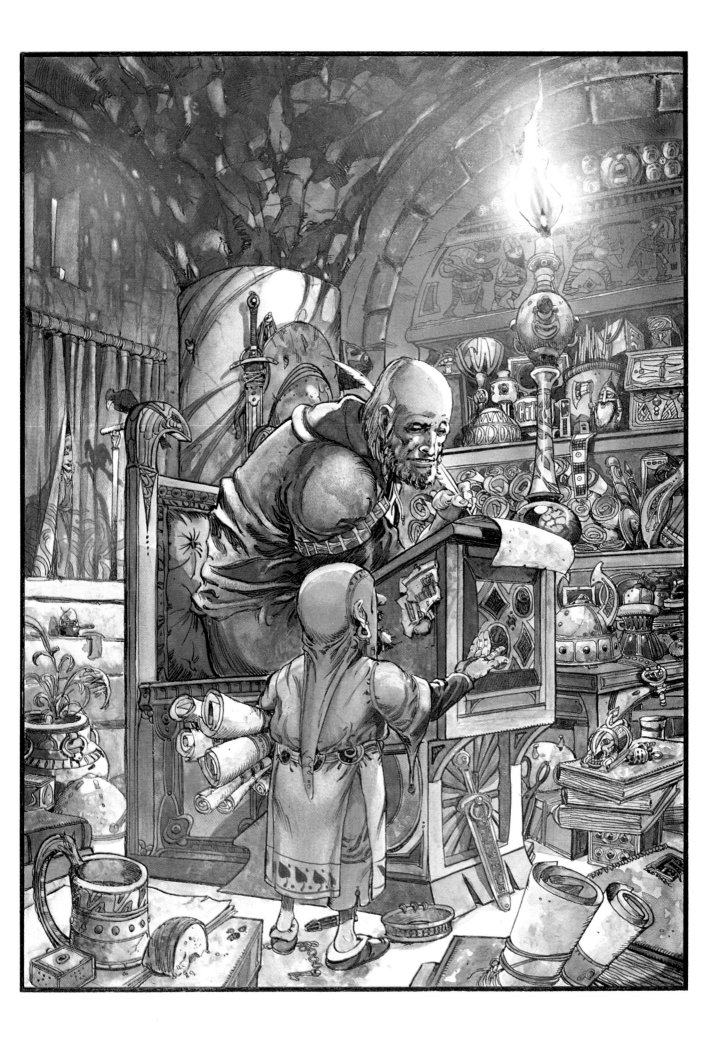

EARLY KINGS

Top Left: Nofret   Bottom Left: Balkar

Center: Aegol

Top Right: Breat & Liffe   Bottom Right: Buld

Kings of the Dwarfs

King Nofret

When the end of the Golden Age had come, King Nofret went to the land of the Pharaohs. The Pharaoh and his people were impressed by Nofret's knowledge. He taught them of stone building and the making of pottery. The Pharaoh saw the fruits of the dwarf culture and he invited all of Nofret's tribe to live under his protection and hospitality. And so the tribe of Nofret came to Egypt.

In Egypt, the dwarfs were free from the problems that were destroying their culture. They devoted their time to building and craftsmanship. Experimenting with new minerals for firing and glazing pottery, they discovered the usefulness of a mineral they named copper.

King Nofret died in glory and was buried in a mighty tomb with all the honors of a pharaoh. The dwarfs of Egypt continued to work with metals after Nofret's death. They learned to make it harder and softer, how to refine it, shape it, and fashion it. The dwarfs made copper tools and jewelry and utensils for the Egyptians. They discovered how to work with gold and silver. Dwarfs who scouted distant lands discovered a metal called tin which they combined with copper to make bronze. Bronze was hard and made the best tools and weapons.

Bronze tools brought the dwarfs a new precision in stone work. Elaborate and demanding new designs were made possible. With Egyptian labor and dwarf craftsmanship, the pyramids and great stone works of Egypt rose in majesty.

The dwarfs taught the Egyptians all they had discovered and the Egyptians learned to work with metal. The important and difficult pieces, though, were left to the superior craftsmanship of the dwarfs.

In time, the tin needed for the making of bronze grew scarce. In the mountains beyond the Middle Sea, the dwarfs found a great supply of tin, but it lay under the ground. A new enterprise was undertaken there, and the dwarfs developed the system of mining. Over the years, many of the dwarfs of Egypt journeyed to the tin mountains to work in the mines. They developed their own forges and smelting furnaces there so as to save them from carrying the tin-bearing rock back to Egypt. For hundreds of years they worked there and became a separate tribe with their own kings.

In the Land of the Pharaohs

The legend of Nofret offers a fascinating solution to an archaeological mystery which has long puzzled Egyptologists. The Tomb of Nofret was opened decades ago, but no logical explanation has ever been offered for the exalted treatment given to this dwarf noble. He was buried with a great treasure in a spectacular tomb.

Dwarfs are frequently depicted in Egyptian art. Wall paintings feature dwarfs at work smelting and casting copper. Dwarfs were employed by the Pharaohs as guards and "curators" of the royal treasures. According to the legend of Nofret, the technology and craftsmanship the dwarfs gave to the Egyptians resulted in the first blossoming of human civilization.

81

Attack of the Aesir Horsemen

Aesir horsemen, the world's first mounted warriors, swept through Europe and the Near East forcing the dwarfs to retreat into the underground spaces of their abandoned mine areas and eventually to migrate to the edges of the continent. For hundreds of years, the dwarfs roamed the world keeping out of the Aesir's reach. Occasionally, the Aesir were able to raid dwarf caravans and take important hostages to ransom for gold or iron weapons. Fleeing the savagery of the Aesir, one group of dwarfs sailed to the island of Britain where they founded the Kingdom of Aegol.

King Balkar

King Balkar led the dwarfs of the Tin Mountains in a time of great change. Deep in the mines, the dwarfs discovered a new metal. Harder than any other metal, it held an edge when sharpened. They called this metal iron and they began to refine it and work with it.

In this time, the land around the Tin Mountains was invaded by savage warriors from the east. These warriors rode horses into battle and they were called the Aesir horsemen. They were the swiftest and most deadly warriors the world had known. The invaders conquered great regions of the world and they cut off the tribe of Balkar from their allies in Egypt.

Balkar moved his tribe and all their furnaces into the abandoned areas of the tin mines. There, Balkar's smiths perfected the making of iron weapons. They learned to mix iron with other substances and to temper it. The dwarfs discovered that swords and axes made of iron

would not bend or dull in battle. Iron shields would resist the blows of any other metal. The workings of iron were kept secret by Balkar's smiths.

In time, the dwarfs of the Tin Mountains assembled an army. They armed themselves with the finest iron weapons. At last they began their escape from the Aesir horsemen. Across the continent they trekked, roaming the world to the west and north. Balkar led

them in their first battles with the Aesir and the dwarf iron prevailed.

The dwarfs carried with them the secret of iron. Everywhere they settled, they dug mines and worked with metals of all kinds, making gold rings and silver utensils and iron weapons. Many kings descended from Balkar's line. One of these was King Niflung, from whom Albrecht descended. Another was King Breat.

Attila and the Niflung

Historical records show that Attila the Hun was a dwarf. The nation of Huns was not a dwarf tribe, so controversy persists as to whether Attila was a renegade dwarf of the ancient race or a stunted man. In the "Lay of the Niflung," an ancient legend of Europe, Attila destroys the Burgundian dynasty in pursuit of the treasure of the Niflung dwarfs. This connection strongly suggests some tie between Attila and the Niflung dwarfs, though none has ever been proved.

Out of the Mountain

Balkar's army lead the dwarfs out of their hiding place in the underground mine tunnels. With iron shields, swords and axes, Balkar's soldiers were the first to challenge the savage Aesir horsemen. Streaming out of the mountainside the army raised a great din of war whoops and battle cries. The horsemen were lured into the rocky terrain of the mountainside where their horses were unable to manuever. In a bloody battle, the dwarfs proved the superiority of iron weapons. Their bravery enabled Balkar's tribe to escape from Central Europe beginning their long trek across the continent.

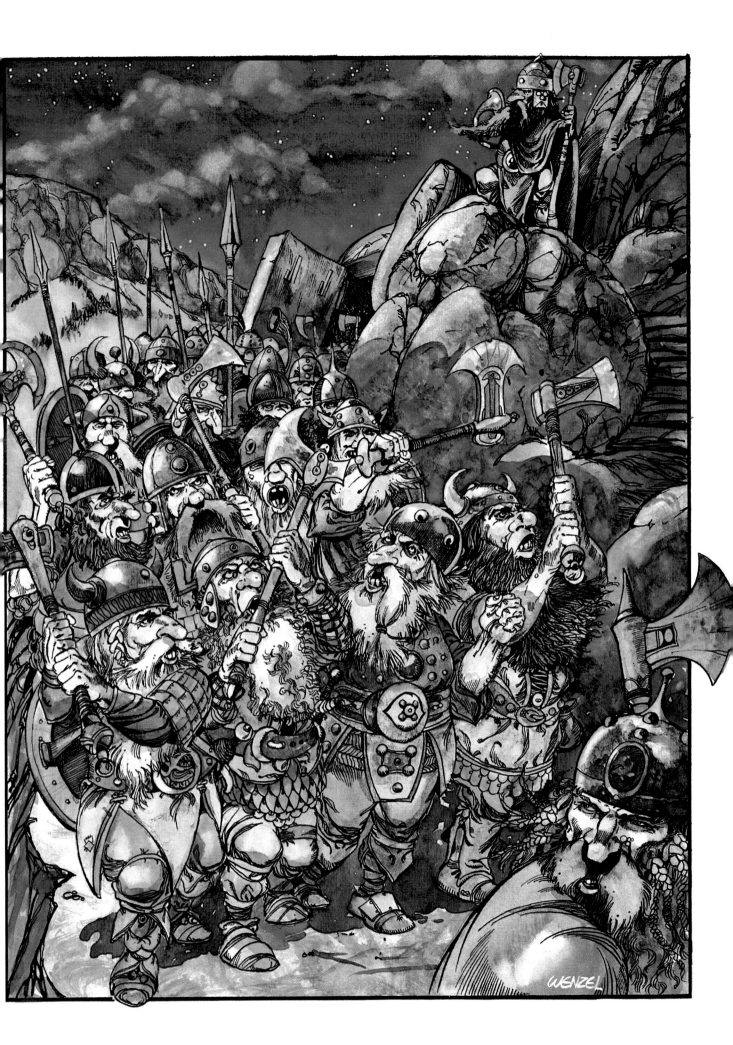

King Breat

The dwarfs of Balkar's line became nomadic, wandering across the continent always out of the Aesir horsemen's reach. At last the dwarfs reached the sea. The King of the dwarfs in these days was Niflung and he decided to continue on until they found the way to the land of Ultima Thule.

One night in the time by the sea, a dwarf woman named Liffe had a dream of dwarfs living in peace on a beautiful island. She told her dream to her husband, a noble dwarf named Breat. Breat decided that he must build a ship and sail in search of this island.

Breat longed for a place away from the horsemen where dwarfs could settle and live in peace. And so he set off in his ship with Liffe and other dwarfs to explore the sea. Their ship was gone only two days. They returned to the camp of the Niflung in jubilation. They had sighted an island which stretched across the whole horizon, and they announced that they would make their homes there. Many of the Niflung dwarfs decided to join them and King Niflung himself blessed their endeavor. And so the Niflung tribe split into two groups. One group remained by the coast building ships while the other continued its travels. The dwarfs who built ships made Breat their King and Liffe their Queen. They soon began to transport their belongings and families across the sea to begin a new life on the island they named Breatland.

On Breatland, the dwarfs discovered the stone observatory of the Golden Age. This was the greatest of lost monuments of that time. The shadows of its great stone arches marked the beginning and the end of the years and the seasons, the days, the months and the alignment of the planets. The dwarfs who built it had disappeared at the end of the Golden Age. It stood now in ruin and disrepair. King Breat directed his subjects in the reconstruction of the monument.

The dwarfs of Breat travelled far and wide over the island. In the north they found a mountainous district rich in metals and covered with timber. There Breat directed his followers to dig mines. In this district the dwarfs settled. Breat lived many years and died with contentment.

Breat's son was named Buld and he became King after his father's death. King Buld was a master at building and mining. Under his direction, the mines descended to great depths and he found new ways to dig into the mountains. Buld invented tools and ways of mining that brought forth better metals. And so it was that Liffe's dream and Breat's quest led to the new life of the dwarfs.

Stonehenge

According to the dwarf legends, Stonehenge was begun in the Golden Age, in a time before the rise of man when dwarfs ruled the earth. Its second phase of construction corresponds to the migration of the dwarfs to Britain around 1500 B.C. as recounted in the story of King Breat. The original designers came solely to build an observatory; no other traces of them have ever been found. Their desire to build an observatory on this exact spot was not discouraged by the absence of stone. The closest outcroppings lay more than thirty miles from the site, indicating that these enormous slabs were transported at least that distance.

This amazing feat of stonework in 3500 B.C. is remarkable, but the knowledge of the planet its builders possessed was even more striking. Scientific testing has proven that the astronomical function required an exact placement on the longitude within an east-west tolerance of less than three miles.

King Aegol

For hundreds of years, the dwarfs of Breatland lived in peace and prosperity. The dwarf
culture flourished and great advances in
metal working were made. At the height of
this era the wisest of the dwarf Kings came to
power and his name was Aegol.

King Aegol foresaw the coming of a new
era. The descendants of the Aesir horsemen
ruled all the continent. They had divided
over the centuries into separate tribes and
made war on each other. Eventually, Aegol
realized, the tribes would come to Breatland.
In preparation, King Aegol began to move his
kingdom underground. With many years of
planning, Aegol designed an underground
civilization that was the largest ever known.
The vast and far-ranging mines had left huge
caverns and long tunnels that were soon filled
with underground dwellings, foundries, and
workshops. King Aegol devised a way to
bring fresh air underground and pipe away
the smoke of the furnaces. He laid out a
beautiful common hall where the dwarfs
could market their wares. He designed a throne
room and feasting rooms and he diverted
streams so that fresh water flowed through
underground fountains and cisterns. He
directed the digging of tunnels which reached
all the way to the sea, and there he kept ships.
And at last his people brought their flourishing civilization underground and established
the Kingdom of Aegol, the name by which it
is known even to this day. And when at last
the tribes of man invaded Breatland, the dwarfs
were safe from harm.

LATE KINGS
Center: Alf

Top Left: Doon-gul   Center Left: Niflung
Bottom: Stor Alf   Top Right: Albrecht
Center Right: Lok   Bottom Right: Weylund

HIGH PRINCES
Center: Mavdor
Top Right: Turold   Bottom Right: Jord, Hinne
Top Left: Gregot   Bottom Left: Lant

Weylund: Last King of Aegol

I. THE ABDUCTION OF ABILYN

Many great Kings ruled the underground
Kingdom after the reign of Aegol. It became
the custom with the Kings to send their sons
abroad to learn of the world and prove their
valor. Such was the intention of King Alf
when he sent his son Lok to Suomi. There Lok
commanded the army of the Niflung dwarfs
in their victory over the Suomi horsemen.
For his conquests, Lok was named King of the
Fyns, a title of honor among the Niflung warriors. When King Alf died on the throne, Lok
returned to his homeland as the new King of
Aegol.

Aegol remained the greatest of all dwarf
kingdoms. It was the site of the best foundry and
metal works in all the world. The metal of Aegol
was famed for its purity and strength. From
his throne, King Lok commanded multitudes
of miners, smiths and alchemists. He knew
every detail of the workings of his Kingdom,
and he ruled wisely but sternly.

King Lok took special care of his wood-cutters. Dwarf woodcutters were a brave and tireless lot. All year long they worked in clearings deep in the forest felling trees for charcoal and timber. From the treetops, the woodcutters had a clear view of the world above. King Lok relied on them to keep watch over the land surrounding Aegol.

One day a woodcutter rushed into King Lok's throne room.

"King Lok," he hailed, "today while your woodcutters toiled in the forest, a most remarkable creature came to us. She is a shepardess named Abilyn, and she is the most beautiful maiden that has ever walked the earth. With promises of golden rings we have brought her here for you to behold."

King Lok was angered by his woodcutters' misdeed, but he held his temper until the maiden was brought before him. She was by far the loveliest woman he had ever seen, a beauty without equal.

And so King Lok connived to make Abilyn his bride. His ministers and all the people objected but none could sway his desire. With riches of gold and silk he courted Abilyn and made her his wife. Abilyn was young and amazed by the underground Kingdom and so she consented to Lok's wishes.

II. WEYLUND'S CURSE

One year after the marriage, Abilyn bore Lok a son and they called him Weylund. He was a beautiful child, but the soothsayers whispered of a curse upon him.

"The child Weylund is half man," said one dwarf soothsayer. "He will sit on the throne of Aegol and deliver the Kingdom into the hands of men."

As the years passed, Abilyn grew tired of her life in the underground Kingdom. The gems and golden rings lost their sparkle for her. She yearned to see the sky again and smell the fresh air. And so when Weylund was ten years old, Abilyn escaped from Aegol to return to her homeland. The beautiful Abilyn was Lok's undoing, for he had ended the pure royal bloodline of Aegol. Weylund his son bore the curse of being Aegol's last King.

III. WEYLUND'S VOYAGE

There was great contention and resentment in Aegol after Abilyn's departure. Whisperings and rumors about the curse of Weylund reached the ears of Lok. And so King Lok decided the time had come for Weylund to be sent out into the world.

Lok arranged for Weylund to study under the twin dwarfs of Sjaeland, Egenrik and Ekenrik. They were a clever devious pair, but they were among the best smiths in the world. Lok would send Weylund to them by his brother Zoral. Weylund would learn the skills he needed and make his mark in the world, then return after he had proved his mettle.

So Weylund and Lok's brother Zoral set off in a small boat. First they sailed in Aegol Bay, the port where dwarf ships harbored. There Zoral taught Weylund seamanship and showed him all the reefs and shallows and the depths and the tides. Then they set off on their journey across the great Cold Sea. Along their way Zoral taught Weylund all of history and geography.

As they crossed the savage sea, Zoral told Weylund stories of the ancient dwarfs. He told him how dwarfs had fashioned the hammer of Thor and how they wove Siff's beautiful golden hair. As they sailed north along the coast of Reidgotaland, Zoral told Weylund about the Aesir horsemen and how they had swept down from the mountains and driven the dwarfs underground. As they sailed south again through the narrow sound between Mälar and the island of Sjaeland, Zoral pointed out that there were as many bays in Mälar as there were headlands in Sjaeland. He explained how the giantess Gefjon had dragged Sjaeland into the sea with her mighty oxen.

At last they reached the tall and blinding white chalk cliffs of southern Sjaeland where Egenrik and Ekenrik awaited them. They secured their boat and climbed the cliffs to a small opening high above the sea. There the clever twins confronted them.

"We will keep Weylund here and teach him what a dwarf should know," they told Zoral. "Return to this place in exactly one year and take him back." With that Zoral was dismissed. He climbed down and waved goodbye to Weylund from the boat. Sadly, Weylund watched his kindly uncle grow smaller and smaller on the glistening sea.

Egenrik and Ekenrik wasted no time in giving Weylund his education. His apprenticeship was difficult and the two dwarfs were severe. They taught him all they knew of smelting, forging, and the making of golden treasures. Weylund was a bright student and soon his cruel masters were delighted to sit and sip mead while Weylund fashioned rings and bracelets, chalices and jewel boxes all for their enrichment. They were secretly amazed at his ability, but they gave him nothing but complaints.

When the year had almost passed, Egenrik and Ekenrik set about an evil scheme. They sealed the opening in the cliff where they had parted with Zoral and opened another one not far away. At the appointed time, the kindly Zoral returned and mounted the white cliff to the new opening.

"Where is Weylund?" he demanded.

"Your memory is bad, old dwarf," the evil twins told him. "We parted on a different spot. This is a brand new opening. Come back in another year and keep your promise this time. Exactly this spot in exactly one year."

Zoral was furious, but he marked the spot well and vowed to return in exactly one year.

And so Weylund spent another year in apprenticeship. In his second year, Weylund learned the dwarf secrets of steel. He learned to fashion axes and knives, daggers and swords, shields and helmets. He worked hard at the forge and anvil and his devious masters gained the worth of his work while they idled away the time.

In this year Weylund learned of Egenrik's and Ekenrik's most carefully guarded secret. Many years before, during the battles with the Aesir horsemen, the dwarf king Albrecht had entrusted the twins with the Niflung treasure. They were sent to hide it and guard it from the horsemen, but instead they kept it for themselves. It was hidden in the chalk cliffs, and only they knew how to find it.

Soon another year had almost passed, and Egenrik and Ekenrik decided to deceive Zoral again. This time Zoral arrived on the appointed day at the appointed place and demanded Weylund's return. No trick or cunning Egenrik and Ekenrik attempted would delay him or misguide him. And so the dark dwarfs, not about to lose their profitable apprentice, toppled a boulder onto Zoral and sent him to his death.

When Weylund heard Egenrik and Ekenrik chuckling over his uncle's death, he vowed to avenge Zoral. To this end, Weylund began his most important metal work.

IV. *THE SWORD* GRAM

"I am going to fashion the perfect sword," Weylund told his masters. They were delighted to think of the price such an item would bring and they encouraged him to begin his labors.

Weylund began by forming a shaft of steel. This shaft he melted, poured, and pounded until it was without flaw. He took the shaft and smashed it on his anvil with all his great strength. If the shaft bent even slightly, he melted it down and started again. This he continued for three months until he had formed a perfect shaft that would not bend or break.

"When will we see this sword?" Egenrik and Ekenrik asked.

"I will bring it to you soon," Weylund answered them.

Weylund spent another three months sharpening the shaft. He took it down to the stream to test it. He would drop a tuft of lamb's wool into the current and hold the sword shaft still in the water. When the wool was cleaved cleanly in two as it floated by he was satisfied.

One night Weylund put silver dust on Egenrik's boots. Then he roused Egenrik from his bed and showed him the sharpened sword shaft. Egenrik swung the shaft at a helmet and the sword cleaved it easily in two. He smashed the sword on an anvil and it would not bend or break.

"An amazing sword!" Egenrik shouted excitedly.

"Yes, but it wants a handle of the very finest gold," Weylund told him.

"You shall have the finest gold in the world," Egenrik told him.

The long hall was flanked on either side by the heads of dragons carved in stone.

Egenrik went straight away down into the secret passages of the chalk clifs just as Weylund had hoped. From the secret treasure room he brought back handfuls of the finest Niflung gold. Unknown to him the silver dust on his boots left a sparkling trail for Weylund to follow.

Certain in his knowledge of the place where the stolen treasure lay, Weylund lovingly finished his sword. When every detail was perfect, Weylund reverently held his awesome weapon aloft.

"Your name shall be *'Gram,'* " he intoned, "and your mission shall be rightful vengeance."

Weylund took *Gram* and entered the chambers of his evil masters.

"Your sword is ready?" they asked excitedly.

"My sword is ready for its final test," Weylund replied, "and that test shall prove how well my sword *Gram* deals in rightful vengeance. If it passes this test, I shall have both your heads in the name of my father's brother, Zoral."

Egenrik and Ekenrik drew their swords, flung spears and axes and furiously tried to outwit Weylund. But no ruse could keep *Gram* from satisfaction and the awesome sword cleaved through shields and sliced the heads of the evil twins cleanly from their necks.

Next Weylund went down into the cliffs by the passage Egenrik's silvered boots had shown him. Through enormous caverns and tiny hallways he followed the silver path until he came to the ancient hall of dragons. The long hall was flanked on either side by the heads of ferocious dragons carved in stone, guarding the secret treasure room. By the head of the last dragon, the silvered footsteps stopped, and in the dragon's mouth Weylund found the key to the treasure room. Weylund left the bulk of the treasure lying there. For himself he carried

only an armful of the Niflung gold. As he prepared to leave he was startled by a dwarf hag. She was very old and had only one eye.

"Who are you, ugly old woman?" Weylund demanded.

"I am the Sybil," she replied. "I was held here by the evil twins until your sword smote off their heads. They prized me like a treasure, for I foretell the future. Now you have freed me, but before I leave this place I shall foretell another future, Weylund."

"Speak it then, old hag," Weylund said. "I have nothing to fear from fate."

"It is not your fortune I speak," the Sybil replied. "It is that of your mighty sword, *Gram.* You have ordained this sword with the blood of vengeance, but the vengeance it has taken against the evil twins was only the first. Twice more shall *Gram* taste sweet revenge." With that the Sybil disappeared into the darkness of the twisted passageways.

V. THE LAND OF THE NJARS

Weylund found the boat that Zoral had sailed still secured by the cliff face. He loaded into it his treasure and his sword and set sail. The breeze blew gently across the sound toward Mälar. Weylund decided to journey there and seek his fortune, the time to return to Aegol had not yet come. So he found a place to his liking called Wolfdale in the land of the Njars. He settled there and lived the life of a dwarf smith.

In Wolfdale, Weylund met a beautiful dwarf maiden named Hervor. He courted her and made for her gold rings set with precious stones. These were the most beautiful rings anyone in the land of the Njars had ever seen. Weylund asked for Hervor's hand in marriage. This she agreed to, provided she received the consent of her father who lived in the far-off land of Burgundia along the river the dwarfs called Granni's road. So Hervor set off to seek her father's consent. Weylund stayed in Wolfdale awaiting her return. While she was away, Weylund fashioned the most beautiful gold ring of all. This was to be the ring with which he would wed his beloved.

The land of the Njars was ruled by the evil and cowardly king Nidud. Word soon reached Nidud that in his kingdom lived a smith whose works were the finest in the land and whose treasures were richer than the king's. One night the king sent out a band of soldiers to steal into Weylund's smithy while Weylund was out hunting boar. They took the ring Weylund had crafted for Hervor and made off with the mighty *Gram.*

When King Nidud examined these treasures, he was astonished at their magnificence. He called his own court smith, a dwarf named Regin, to explain how the dwarf Weylund had a treasure finer than his own.

"Perhaps he is a thief," guessed Regin, "and has stolen someone else's treasure. Bring him here and test him and let the truth be known." And so Nidud sent his soldiers back that very night.

When Weylund returned from hunting, he sensed a loss. He quickly discovered the theft of *Gram* and the golden ring. Weylund slumped before the fire. He mourned the loss of Hervor's ring; the loss of *Gram* left him feeling defenseless. He roasted the boar and drank draft after draft of mead, then fell asleep before the fire. He awoke as Nidud's soldiers fastened him in fetters and bore him off.

From his home in Wolfdale, Weylund was brought to the court. There he appeared before Nidud and was enraged to find *Gram* hanging by the coward's side. He saw the ring he had fashioned for his wife on the hand of Bodvild, Nidud's young daughter. Regin came and stood beside Weylund.

"There shall be a contest between Regin and Weylund to determine who shall be smith to the king," Nidud declared. "Weylund, you shall make a sword and Regin, you shall make a shield. You shall meet at this place in one month and decide the contest with blows."

Weylund and Regin set about their tasks. Regin worked at his own smithy with his familiar tools, but Weylund was left to learn the peculiarities of the forge that was given him. One night after two weeks had passed, Regin stole into Weylund's forge while Weylund slept. There he found the shaft of the sword that Weylund was making. This he took and cast into the sea.

The next morning Weylund stood at the door of Regin's forge. "Where is the shaft you stole?" he asked.

"Perhaps you've hammered it so thin it's slipped your vision," Regin laughed. "Better you should spend your time preparing for your downfall than darkening my door with your prattle, Weylund."

For the next two weeks Weylund worked by day and night; his forge burned white hot and never cooled. The hammering kept the hounds awake and their howling annoyed Regin.

On the eve of the contest, Weylund carried the sword down to the stream. He sharpened it in the manner of *Gram*, working and reworking it until he could hold it in the stream and cleave in two a piece of floating lamb's wool.

On the appointed day, Weylund and Regin appeared at the court. Nidud and his guests gathered round in celebration. Banners and bunting were hung and great horns sounded to announce the contest.

Regin proudly displayed his massive shield of steel, hobbed and thick. It looked able to withstand the blow of a giant. The court of Nidud applauded. Weylund then raised his sword with both his hands above his head. It shone beautifully and the court of Nidud gasped as it came suddenly singing down and carved the shield of Regin, the helmet of Regin, and the head of Regin all neatly in two.

So Weylund was brought before Nidud's throne and appointed court smith.

"I do not desire this," Weylund announced to the king. "I have slain a fellow dwarf for your amusement and now I will depart your land."

But Nidud ordered Weylund seized and hamstrung and placed on the island of Jernild. There a forge was built for him and he was held in captivity to fashion treasures for the court.

Weylund was crippled forever and he hobbled around working at his smithy. He never complained about his captivity, but busied himself fashioning countless treasures for the court of Nidud. He made Nidud seven great swords and seven matching daggers and seven battle axes and seven polished shields. Nidud had so many glorious weapons to show off that he no longer carried *Gram*, but left it in his chamber to gather dust. For Nidud's wife, Weylund fashioned gold jewelry and candlesticks and jewel-encrusted boxes and plates and handmirrors and chests full of sparkling baubles such as no kingdom had ever seen. Word of the greatness of Nidud's smith, Weylund, reached in all directions to kingdoms far and wide.

Weylund raised his sword above his head and the court of Nidud gasped as it came suddenly singing down and carved the shield of Regin and the helmet of Regin and the head of Regin all neatly in two.

VI. BODVILD

King Nidud's daughter Bodvild grew from the child who had worn Weylund's ring into a beautiful princess. Her hair was thick and golden and her eyes sparkled like cut gems. Knights and princes came great distances to court her, but she was melancholy and spurned them all before they could present their gifts. Nidud arranged jousts and contests for his daughter's pleasure so she might be impressed by the bravery of her suitors, but Bodvild had only disgust for these spectacles.

She sat day after day spinning and weaving, surrounded by unwanted gifts. The only possession she valued was the beautiful ring that Weylund had fashioned for his bride. She sat one day admiring it. The ring no longer fit her finger. It was made for the hand of a dwarf maiden and had fit just right when she was a child. Bodvild took the ring to Nidud and asked him to have Weylund enlarge it. But Nidud was so unhappy with his daughter's refusal of worthy suitors that he spitefully denied this simple request.

So the lovely Bodvild decided to visit Weylund on her own. She stole away one night in a little boat and rowed to Jernild. Other than the king's soldiers, she was Weylund's first visitor, and he received her gladly.

"You have grown so beautiful," Weylund greeted her. She showed him the ring and made her request. Weylund took the ring tenderly. He explained to her the story of his beloved Hervor and how he came to fashion the ring for their wedding day. His story touched Bodvild deeply and she began to weep at her selfishness. Weylund comforted her and they spent many hours in warm conversation.

"Although this ring is my only prized possession," Bodvild said, "I must leave it here with you."

"If the ring brings you joy," Weylund countered, "then I shall fit it for you. For me it holds only painful memories." He took her hand then to fit it and such a wave of tenderness engulfed them that they embraced passionately.

Bodvild's visits were frequent after that night, and she became enchanted with the kingly half-dwarf, Weylund. Her hand bore his ring forever after.

VII. NIDUD'S SONS

Nidud had two sons, Alvor and Alved. They were mean and quarrelsome youths much like their father, and Nidud loved them deeply. One morning before dawn, the two boys went down to the sea to fish. There, they encountered their sister Bodvild, on her way back from a visit to Jernild.

"So, you're having the dwarf make you treasures of your own!" they cried. Bodvild hid her true feelings and instead confessed to their charge. She ceased her visits to Jernild for fear of her father's wrath.

The two boys decided to visit Weylund and secretly acquire treasures themselves. So they rowed out to Jernild late one night and found the dwarf at his forge. They looked around his workshop and found a carved chest with a heavy lock.

That must be where the finest treasures of all are kept, they agreed, and demanded that Weylund open it and given them its contents. They had no fear of Weylund for he hobbled so slowly they were sure he could never harm them.

"Gathering dust in your father's chamber is an old sword of mine," Weylund told them. "Bring it to me tomorrow and I will give you the contents of the chest." The greedy boys agreed readily, and then departed as the winter wind began to whistle mournfully. Weylund sat by the embers of his forge, as outside a storm brewed and snow began to fall on Jernild.

Weylund's thoughts were interrupted by something in the wind. He wrapped himself and limped outside. From the end of the little dock he watched sheets of snow melt into the salty waves. Then he heard it again, his name in the wind. He peered into the storm and he saw a light at sea, a ship. He hurried back into

his quarters and lit a lantern which he carried to the end of the dock. There he stood swinging his lantern, wondering what ship had come to Jernild and what voice was calling his name.

The ship anchored and a skiff came rowing to his dock. As it approached he recognized the sailors as dwarfs, two rowing and one old dwarf in the stern. Weylund welcomed them and brought them inside. He stoked the fire and handed his shivering guests cups of mead. The two rowers sat huddled by the fire. The third

dwarf was a noble, white-haired fellow. Weylund approached him and introduced himself,
"I am Weylund, son of Lok, and this is the forge
built for me by Nidud, King of the Njars. I am
held here against my will to fashion treasures
for his court."

"I am Albrecht, King of the Niflung," began
the white-haired dwarf. "We have sought you
for many years since we heard of your exploits
on Sjaeland.

"Many years ago your former masters, Egenrik and Ekenrik, stole the Niflung treasure they
had been entrusted to guard. Though we knew
of their presence on Sjaeland, we were unable
to capture them or find their secret vaults in
the chalk cliffs. They were a wily pair, but their
greed at last undid them. Your beloved Hervor
brought us the story of your vengeance and your
discovery of the secret room in the cliffs. When
Hervor came seeking her father's permission
to marry, we returned to Wolfdale in her stead.
We would have brought you back to the land of
the Niflung and made you a member of our
court in return for your assistance. Instead we
found your home deserted and ransacked and
we thought you dead. Hervor mourned you for
two years and then died of grief.

"In recent time we heard stories about the
richness of Nidud's court and the appearance
there of legendary swords. Our spies discovered the details of your imprisonment and
so we have come to trade our help for yours.
Take us to the secret vaults in the chalk cliffs of
Sjaeland and we will free you from your imprisonment."

"And what then?" Weylund asked.

"Then you have a choice,"· Albrecht explained. "You may return with us to join the
court of the Niflung, you may go your own way
as you see fit, or . . . " Albrecht hesitated.

"Or what?" Weylund prodded.

"Or you may try to set order in your father's
house."

"What is the trouble in my father's house?"

"Your father is very ill, he may already be
dead." Albrecht measured Weylund and continued. "You are his only heir. The ministers
of Aegol speak of a curse, and they are contend-
ing for the throne of Aegol themselves."

"I am Lok's heir. The time has come at last
for me to return and rule Aegol," Weylund
stated.

"You have the temperament of a king,"
Albrecht cautioned, "but you no longer have
the body of a warrior."

"In my left hand I will wield a crutch," Weylund answered, "in my right I shall wield *Gram.*"

"Even your famous *Gram* cannot withstand
an army of Aegol's warriors," Albrecht
reasoned.

"How many warriors man your ship?"
Weylund asked.

"There are but a hundred."

"Then you will commit them to my service,"
Weylund demanded.

"That is a large order from a crippled king in
exile," Albrecht said angrily.

"It is a large treasure," Weylund smiled.
"Hide your ship and return in two days. We
shall sail for Aegol where you will aid me in
my claim, then at last I will tell you how to find
your treasure."

"It is as one Dwarf King in assistance to another that I enter this alliance," Albrecht stated,
"and not as hostage to a treasure."

"And so shall our agreement be honored,"
Weylund concluded.

Albrecht returned to his ship and Weylund
remained awake all through the night plotting
the events of the next two days.

VIII. THE SECOND VENGEANCE OF GRAM

The storm had ended and the day dawned on a calm grey sea. Weylund looked out at the fresh cover of snow blanketing Jernild. In the distance he saw a boat approaching. The conniving sons of Nidud were keeping their appointment.

Patiently he waited for them to stomp into his forge. Brazenly they pushed open the door and flung *Gram* onto the floor.

"Here is your dusty sword, old dwarf. Now open the chest and be quick about it, for we must return to prepare for tomorrow's feast," they demanded.

"But wait," Weylund said. "The chest contains a great treasure and a smaller one. We must decide which of you shall take the lion's share."

The two boys eyed each other in rivalry.

"I am the older, it will be mine," said Alvor.

"No, we must have a contest," countered Alved. "That is the way of our kingdom."

"What contest then?" challenged Alvor.

"This contest shall decide," said Weylund: "You will climb down the dock outside the door onto the beach. You will walk along the beach to the great rock at the other end of the island. Then you will have a foot race running backwards from there to here and I will judge the winner."

"A footrace running backwards?" protested Alvor. "What kind of contest is that?"

"This is the way dwarfs decide these things," his brother answered. "Let's get on with it."

And so they walked along the beach where the waves washed the shore until they reached the rock and then they started their backwards race. Weylund watched them while he admired *Gram*. He unsheathed the sword and swung it through the air, listening to it sing. As the boys approached he held *Gram* behind his back. They finished their race in a dead heat.

"It's a tie," Weylund announced as they came into the forge, "and so you must both have the same prize." As they eagerly pushed forward toward the chest, Weylund steadied himself with a crutch in his his left hand and raised *Gram* with his right.

"And your prize shall also be a reward for the hospitality your father has shown me." And he sliced off both their heads with one swoop of his sword.

Weylund hid the two bodies beneath the ashes of his forge. From their skulls he scraped the hair and made from them two feasting bowls set in silver. All this he accomplished before the next day when Nidud's soldiers came to collect the special treasure for the feast.

When the soldiers arrived they found the boat. "Have you seen Nidud's sons?" they asked.

"They said they came to hunt a white seal that lives on the great rock across the island. Perhaps you'll find them there," Weylund answered.

The soldiers found two sets of footprints in the snow leading from Weylund's forge to the rock, but they found no other footprints and no sign of Nidud's sons. They took the feasting bowls and other treasures along with the boat of Nidud's sons and returned to tell Nidud that his sons had disappeared into the sea.

Late in the day Albrecht's ships appeared. Weylund was ready and he carried *Gram* at his side. In the daylight Weylund saw that Albrecht's ship was a strong dwarf warship, and the ship was named *Wings*. The skiff came to the dock and Weylund was carried aboard.

"We sail first to Nidud's royal docks," Weylund commanded.

"I have agreed to help you at Aegol to gain your rightful place as heir to Lok," Albrecht protested. "But I have not agreed to fight the Njars with just one ship."

"There will be no fight," Weylund promised.

And so they sailed the short distance to Nidud's docks by the palace where the feast was under way. They stopped short of the dock and lined the ship's rail with gleaming shields.

"Send Nidud down to the dock," Weylund hailed a soldier who stood there. "Tell him Weylund has come to call."

The feast was interrupted. Nidud and his court came down to the dock in all their finery, still carrying their feasting bowls full of mead.

"I have come to announce my departure, Nidud," Weylund called. "Your soldiers are drunk with mead and we will be gone before you can man a ship."

"Your escape is made," Nidud answered. "But grant me please the whereabouts of my sons if you know what has happened to them."

"That I will grant, if you grant me something in turn," Weylund offered.

"Name it and it is given," Nidud pledged.

"And you must swear by sword's edge, by shield's rim, by ship's keel that you will make true your offer."

"I swear by sword's edge, by shield's rim, by ship's keel that I will grant you your request if you tell me the whereabouts of my sons," Nidud swore.

"Here is my request. You will go to your daughter Bodvild and you will find her heavy with my child. That child you shall raise as your own," Weylund told him.

Nidud was struck with grief and sent for Bodvild. "If this be true I shall honor my word," Nidud shouted. "Now where are my sons?"

"Send your men to the forge on Jernild. The forge your folly built is spattered with your sons' blood, their bodies lie under the ashes. Their skulls I scraped and set in silver for your feasting cup. Drink to their memory, Nidud!" And Weylund sailed away.

Nidud gasped in horror and dropped the cup full of mead. Bodvild came then and he queried her. Bodvild confessed that Weylund's words were true.

"Against his wiles, I had no will to struggle," Bodvild told her father. To her was born a daughter, Vidge, and Nidud made good his promise to raise the child as his own.

Weylund led the twenty-five brave dwarfs into battle aboard the warship Wings.

IX. THE RETURN TO AEGOL

Across the sea Weylund and Albrecht sailed in the great ship *Wings*. A steady wind and an untroubled sea made swift their journey. As they sailed, Albrecht told Weylund of the plight of Aegol.

"The petty kings and barons of Briton have long fought their battles among themselves. Seldom have the dwarfs in their underground fortress at Aegol been disturbed by these struggles. But in the present day, with King Lok disabled, the dwarfs of Aegol have become contentious. The fight amongst themselves and leave the riches of Aegol undefended.

"Among the petty Briton kings there has risen one cruel and clever ruler. His name is Uther Pendragon and he seeks to rule all of Briton. His men are many and they prowl the land and the sea, raiding villages they claim to protect. Pendragon lusts after good dwarf gold and dwarf-made arms. I fear that without a strong leader, the dwarfs of Aegol will succumb to his savage might."

Albrecht related many stories of Pendragon's treachery to Weylund. Weylund resolved to unify the dwarfs of Aegol and looked forward to the journey's end.

At last land was sighted. Weylund recognized the coast.

"We are just north of the Aegol bay where dwarf ships are kept," Weylund announced. "Sail south along the shore to yonder hilly point. Around the point and we are home."

And so the seawise dwarfs brought *Wings* close to shore and sailed south. *Wings* was a ship of Viking design, broad amidships and drawing only four feet of water. As they reached the point an alarm went up.

"Fire!" yelled the lookout.

They halted their progress and watched thick black clouds of smoke billow from the other side of the hilly point.

"Send a scout ashore, have him climb the point," Weylund ordered. And so they lay at anchor awaiting the scout's return.

"I fear that Pendragon's ships are attacking Aegol," Albrecht whispered to Weylund.

"When will the tide be lowest?" Weylund asked the navigator.

"Just before sunset," the navigator reported.

Soon the scout returned and gave his report. "Two great warships of the flag of Pendragon have set fire to the dwarf ships in Aegol bay," he shouted. "They are preparing to attack. Three hundred warriors man these two ships."

"We are outnumbered, we must flee," said Albrecht.

"No," answered Weylund, "I have a plan. Take seventy-five dwarf warriors ashore and proceed to a secret entrance to Aegol which I shall describe. With the remaining dwarf warriors I shall attack Pendragon's ships. You will tell the dwarfs of Aegol that you lead them under my command. Just before sunset you will attack the bay with all the warriors of Aegol you can muster along with your own seventy-five good men."

"I cannot lead my warriors to slaughter," Albrecht announced. "They are the sons of my kingdom. And you cannot defeat two of Pendragon's warships in a single ship with only twenty-five dwarf warriors."

"We shall defeat them," Weylund answered, "and we shall not lose a single dwarf."

So Albrecht went bravely ashore and led his men to the secret entrance Weylund had described. Weylund sat calmly while *Wings* rocked gently in the waves, straining at anchor.

Overhead a seahawk attacked a flock of
screaming gulls.

"The gulls have found the hawk's nest,"
said Weylund.

Weylund sent ten men ashore to collect pitch.
Aboard the ship he stoked a great fire in the
firepot. As sunset approached they weighed
anchor and began to round the point.

"Dip your arrows in pitch," Weylund commanded. "We will rain fire on the warships
with the seawind at our back."

Across from the point and out to sea lay a
small rocky island. The navigator turned
to Weylund.

"Do you know these waters well?" he asked.

"Very well," smiled Weylund. "Between the
island and the point the sea is six feet deep at
low water. Deep enough for *Wings* to sail
unhindered."

"And shallow enough to run a Briton warship
aground," the navigator beamed.

Twenty-five dwarf warriors stood ready with
bows as *Wings* rounded the point on a hard
tack. Pendragon's men had begun to go ashore
in skiffs. Fifty men stood ready on the shore.
Skiffs were shuttling back and forth as *Wings*
came into sight. The Britons were thrown into
confusion as *Wings* drew close.

"Fire your arrows!" Weylund commanded.
The dwarfs fired their flaming arrows with
the sea breeze at their backs. The Britons
fired back, but their arrows fell short in the wind.
The warships weighed anchor and set sail to
give chase. Parts of the ships were already in
flames. The warships couldn't sail into the wind
toward *Wings* so they turned and tacked south.

"They're fleeing," the navigator guessed.

"They will turn and try to cut off our tack
behind the island," Weylund said. "Turn *Wings*
into the wind and wait."

As *Wings* lay luffing, the warships turned and bore down on the dwarfs from seaward. Now Pendragon's men were ready with flaming arrows and the wind at their backs. *Wings* turned and tacked hard, racing the warships for the water between the point and the island. The warships closed in, forcing *Wings* toward shore. The Briton warriors screamed their bloodthirsty war cries.

On the beach at Aegol Bay the fifty Briton warriors watching the battle at sea were surprised by a superior force of dwarfs led by Albrecht. They were slaughtered with not a single dwarf casualty. Now the dwarfs lined the crest of the point watching the drama of the twenty-five brave dwarfs under Weylund pursued by Pendragon's ships.

Pendragon's warships were faster, bigger, and better armored than the open *Wings*, but they drew nine feet of water fully loaded. The warships sailed behind the island, closing in on *Wings* at top speed. The Briton war cries turned suddenly to cries of terror as the first warship ran aground at full speed. Timbers exploded, the mast snapped like a twig, and the Briton warriors sank like stones. The second warship saw the trap, but went aground with an awful groan of bursting timbers as the frantic sailors tried to turn her. Pendragon's forces were vanquished.

On the shore and all along the hill crest the dwarfs of Aegol cheered Weylund's victory and welcomed home their King.

X. WEYLUND, KING OF AEGOL

Weylund was carried triumphant into the halls of Aegol. The ministers drew round him and made a pronouncement.

"Weylund, son of Lok, you are the rightful heir to the throne of Aegol. Many have contended that you carry your mother's curse and that you would deliver us into the hands of men who are our enemies. Now you have returned in our hour of need and saved us from them. We beg your forgiveness for our doubts. You are a great warrior. And you shall be a great King. Hail King Weylund!"

The coronation of Weylund was a magnificent event. The doors of Aegol were opened to all. Albrecht and his men stayed for the celebration.

During his reign, Weylund succeeded in uniting all the factions of Aegol. Under his leadership, the dwarfs became strong. Uther Pendragon and his men never again dared to challenge the dwarf Kingdom.

For many years all was well in Aegol. But as Weylund grew older, contention began again to plague the Kingdom of the Dwarfs. Weylund was without heir and the question of who should succeed him on the throne of Aegol was disputed bitterly. Rival factions made their claims and counter claims. Fights erupted in the court and the aging Weylund was pressed to make a decision on the matter.

So Weylund retired to a secret cave with *Gram*, the symbol of his reign. There he contemplated for several days the state of the Kingdom and the kind of king necessary to keep it whole. He thought of the greedy ministers who plotted to take over Aegol for their own enrichment.

At last he rose. He unsheathed *Gram* and dropped his crutches.

"*Gram* shall decide who shall be King," he pronounced. And he drove the mighty sword deep into a stone.

XI. GRAM'S *THIRD VENGEANCE*

Weylund had sword and stone brought before his court, where a bewildered gathering assembled.

"Whosoever shall draw the sword from the stone shall be the rightful king," he swore.

Every minister, every noble, and every knave in all of Aegol came then into the hall and all attempted to draw the sword from the stone. None were successful.

Weylund watched from the throne as dwarf after dwarf failed the test. When every dwarf had failed, a tall figure in a hooded cape came forward from the shadows.

"Hail Weylund and the court of Aegol!" he said. All assembled there fell silent.

"I am Merlin the sorcerer and I have been summoned here to tell you of your new king. You have sworn that the next rightful king shall be he who draws the sword from the stone, Weylund. There is only one in the world who can do so, and he is man, not dwarf."

A murmur went up in the hall at the pronouncement of the sorcerer. Merlin continued, "His name is Arthur, and with your oath you have delivered your Kingdom into his hands. This, Weylund, is the third vengeance of *Gram* prophesized by the Sybil of Sjaeland. It is the vengeance of your mother Abilyn and it is your birth curse. Arthur shall reign over dwarfs and knights and all the factions of Briton. You may despise his ilk, for his father is Uther Pendragon, but he will be the greatest king that Aegol and Briton will know."

Sadly, the dwarfs listened, knowing Merlin's words to be truth. They escorted him and the sword in the stone to a far-off town where Arthur waited. A dwarf minister stood at Arthur's side as he withdrew *Gram*. A dwarf minister sat at Arthur's round table. Aegol served King Arthur well, equipping him and his knights with the finest arms and treasures. And for his part, Arthur was indeed the greatest king Aegol ever served.

And thus the deceit of Abilyn, the curse of Weylund, and the third vengeance of *Gram* brought an end to the lineage of dwarf kings.

124

*"Whosoever shall draw the sword from the stone
shall be the rightful king," vowed Weylund.*

The Dwarfs and King Arthur

Under the leadership of Arthur, the united Britons repelled waves of invaders who sought to conquer the island. After Arthur's death, the union of Britons fell. The splintered groups of Briton warrior's proved no match for the invasion of savage Angles who landed in the North and seized control. Next the Saxons came, warriors followed by whole families of settlers. The invaders built their farms and villages and drove the Britons to the far reaches of the island. The struggle for power between the bands of invaders was bitterly fought. Kings came to power and new kings soon replaced them. The control of England, as it came to be called, shifted from hand to hand. Throughout this period, the dwarfs of Aegol in their underground kingdom remained unvanquished, and the influence of the dwarf princes became an important element in politics.

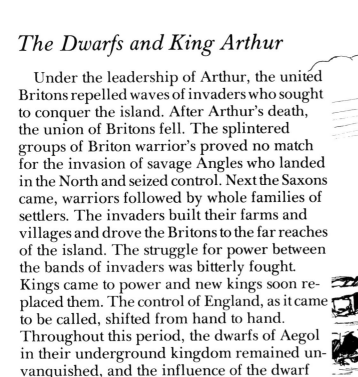

Turold the Messenger

THE BAYEAUX TAPESTRY

After the Norman Conquest, Bishop Odo commissioned a tapestry depicting the events leading up to the battle of Hastings. This unique historical record hangs to this day in the Bayeaux Cathedral in Normandy. In the Bayeaux tapestry, Turold is shown taking a message to Count Guy demanding Harold Godwinson's transfer. Turold's name, along with those of the most important figures in the account, is written out above his head. His stature in the tapestry definitely shows him as a dwarf. His hair is cut in the Norman style with the back of the head shaved. This probably is an inaccuracy intended to symbolize his allegiance to Normandy.

TUROLD, TWELFTH PRINCE OF AEGOL

After the tragic reign of Weylund, the dwarfs were without a king, governing themselves by the election of princes. The Angles, the Saxons and all England's inhabitants were loath to disturb the Kingdom of Aegol. Only the Vikings dared enter the region, and they came not to conquer, but to barter. The dwarfs remained the world's best smiths, and the Vikings honored nothing more highly than finely-honed steel. So it was that Canute the Great, the mighty Danish Viking, sent an emissary to Aegol seeking dwarf weapons and the blessings of the prince for his invasion of England. The deal was struck and the dwarfs profited from the years of Viking rule.

Hrolf the Walker, whom the French came to know as Rollo, first duke of Normandy, visited Aegol before he made his invasion of the French coast. He too traded for weapons in the Royal Hall of Aegol. And so the Duchy of Normandy and the descendants of Canute and the dwarfs of Aegol came to be allied.

In the reign of Mavdor, the eleventh prince of Aegol, uncertainty retained its hold over England's future. Mavdor sent his son Turold and his beautiful daughter Matilda to the court of Normandy for their education. There they became friends of William the Bastard, heir to the Duke of Normandy. William became enamored of the beautiful dwarf Matilda and they were married.

After Mavdor's death, Turold was elected the twelfth prince of Aegol. In the early days of his reign, Turold acted as a liaison for Edward the Confessor, heir to Canute the Great, the last Dane to rule England. Through a compromise with the powerful Saxons, Edward was crowned King of England. By the terms of the agreement Turold arranged, Edward consented to marry the daughter of Earl Godwin, the leader of the Saxons, in return for their support. For his part in these negotiations Turold earned a reputation for being a shrewd political dealer, and, because of his ability to represent the case of others, he became known as Turold the Messenger.

Edward was successful in taking the throne, but his reign was troubled. His marriage, arranged to give England a new bloodline, bore no heirs. Edward withdrew from the demands of power, becoming a religious king. The Godwins made a mockery of his rule. While Godwin's armies brazenly marauded his land, Edward spent his days planning a majestic cathedral at Westminster.

In his later years Edward retaliated by choosing William of Normandy as his successor. This pronouncement enraged the Godwins. As Edward lay dying, the Godwin family plotted to take the throne. The savage Harold, Earl Godwin's second son, was selected to succeed Edward. This selection was contested by Tostig, Godwin's eldest son, the Earl of Northumbria. For his objections, Tostig was removed from his earldom.

The brutal Saxon clan flouted the solemn agreement which Turold had forged and Turold protested their treachery. So it was with great surprise that Turold received a request from Tostig, the eldest son of Godwin, for a secret meeting.

In a location of Turold's choosing, Tostig confided the Saxon plot to place the warrior Harold on the throne.

"William of Normandy will never allow Harold to usurp the throne," Turold told Tostig.

"You may be wrong," Tostig countered. "Harold is planning to sail to Normandy to find a way to convince your brother-in-law to stay out of England."

"This is a strange time for you to turn traitor, Tostig. What is your motive in coming to me?" asked the dwarf prince.

Tostig reddened. "Justice is my motive," he said angrily. "Northumbria has been taken from me. I seek my rightful earldom, nothing more. I sail now to the north to seek Viking allies. Aegol must arm us and warn William of my brother's plans."

Turold nodded, stroking his beard, his shrewd eyes on the Saxon. At last he answered. "We will arm your expedition, Tostig, but we must be sure we do not arm a hostile force. If you enlist a Viking king, send him to Aegol where we will deliver arms to him." Tostig agreed to this simple condition and left encouraged, bound for the north. By accepting his condition, Tostig had convinced Turold there was no trick or treachery.

Turold repaired to a cave in the mountains where he considered the ambitions of Tostig, Harold and William. He contemplated the fate of England and the role of the dwarfs in the battles which would soon be fought. After a day and a night, Turold the Messenger emerged. He ordered a ship be prepared and loaded with Aegol's finest arms. Disguised in the hooded capes of common fishermen, Turold and his bodyguard set sail for Normandy. Along with the gleaming dwarf-crafted weapons, Turold carried a carefully-wrought plan for the defeat of Harold and the hated Saxons.

Beneath a massive oak in a meadow on the Normandy shore, Turold and his bodyguards spread their cargo of shining arms. Turold ordered his men to climb the tree and watch for intruders while a messenger went to William's court. There they waited for William, Duke of Normandy and Turold's brother-in-law. William arrived with Norman guards and his brother, the Bishop Odo.

Turold hailed him, saying, "William of Normandy, friend, ally, and husband of my sister, the Saxons seek to usurp your throne. I bring you weapons and a plan to conquer England."

131

William's soldiers were eager to inspect the fabled arms of Aegol. As they kneeled to inspect them, Bishop Odo halted the warriors, proclaiming: "No Norman shall touch these heathen arms before they have been blessed for our use." Odo prepared himself for a benediction.

Turold was enraged by this insult. "Have you finished your magic incantation?" he chided the Bishop.

"Beware, little heathen, lest my magic take your head for blasphemy," seethed the Bishop.

The Normans had not noticed the dwarf guard above them in the oak tree. "Beware yourself, pompous prelate, lest a host of heathen angels bear you away to hell," Turold replied, summoning his soldiers to a chorus of hoots and catcalls. Bishop Odo cowered in surprise while Turold laughed heartily. William restrained his brother, but not before the Bishop had vowed vengeance upon the wily dwarf prince. The Normans gathered the weapons and the combined party returned to William's court.

William and Turold met privately and Turold gave William his plan.

"Edward the Confessor is ill and near death. His marriage to Godwin's daughter bore no heir and so Edward has named you his successor. The Saxons rage that they have no connection to the throne and so they conspire to place their favorite warrior, Harold Godwinson, on the throne in your place. But Harold is the second son of Earl Godwin. Godwin's first son, Tostig, has objected and they have taken away his Earldom in Northumbria. The Vikings will support him, it providing them with a good excuse to loot the towns they conquer. The dwarfs will arm their expedition."

With battle axes and shields, the dwarfs armed the Viking force. To the Viking
King they presented gold riches and a mighty sword.

"Must I defeat two pups of the Saxon bitch to have my rightful throne?" William objected.

"No, William, hear my plan. When Tostig and the Vikings attack from the North, Harold will march to meet them. In his absence, you will cross the channel, gathering supplies and building fortresses along the undefended coast. Only one army will emerge from the battle of the brothers. If it be Tostig, he will compromise for some feifdom in Northumbria. If it be Harold, you must defeat him." William nodded in understanding. "Do not attack until the Vikings have landed," said Turold, "and your victory will be assured."

"What does Harold know of these approaching battles?" William wondered.

"Harold plans to somehow trick you into an allegiance before you learn of his plans. Of his brother's treachery he knows nothing."

"So the Vikings will attack Harold by surprise; he will be either defeated or weakened, and opposition to my army will be slight," said William, savoring this advantage. "You serve us well, Turold. The dwarfs of Aegol will not be forgotten."

After his audience with Turold, William met with his brother.

"It is clear, Bishop Odo, we must conquer England to take the throne. Turold and the dwarfs have given us an advantage in arms and an excellent plan of attack. Unbeknownst to Harold, his brother Tostig will attack from the north with a force of Vikings. When Harold marches to meet them, we will make our landing unchallenged."

"I must take our plan to the Pope and the Christian kings," said Odo. "Our invasion of England must be presented as an expansion of the Holy Roman Empire. But I fear the Christian kings will frown on an alliance with the Vikings."

"We are but six generations from Norway," William chuckled. "We are Vikings ourselves."

"But we are not heathens," said Odo without humor.

"No, and neither shall we be allied to them," William continued, "as we are not allied to the sea or the forests or the mountains that figure in our battles. We shall know their dispositions and put them to our use. Thus you will represent our plan to the Christian kings."

To this logic Odo agreed and he added: "By the same measure shall we put the dwarfs to use."

William nodded, silently accepting his brother's statement. William had more sympathy for the Vikings than for the church, but he knew the influence of the church would grow as surely as the Viking empire would decline. Though his wife was a dwarf, William knew that alliance, too, would be sacrificed to the interests of the church. The dwarfs and the Vikings who would assist the Norman Conquest were aiding in their own ruin. They would be called heathens and be banished from England under Christian rule.

Bishop Odo left on his journey to Rome. Soon afterward came a message from William's neighbor, Count Guy. Harold Godwinson had been blown ashore in a storm and taken captive by Guy's soldiers. William summoned Turold to discuss this strange turn of events.

"Harold's mission to strike an alliance is off to a poor start," Turold smirked.

"Shall we allow Count Guy to hold him for ransom?" William wondered.

"No," said Turold. "Let me take a message to Count Guy. I will demand he release Harold to your custody."

"And what then?" asked William.

"We will turn the tables on his mission," Turold schemed. "You will demand that Harold recognize the wish of Edward that you shall assume the throne."

"And then release him?" William objected.

"Yes," insisted Turold, "release him to honor his oath and save the bloodshed, or break it and suffer the wrath of you and your church. If you continue to hold him prisoner, the Saxons will attack Normandy and cause destruction to your duchy while Tostig and the Vikings conquer England."

William agreed to this plan and Turold went with two Norman lancers to the court of Count Guy to secure Harold's transfer. Count Guy agreed and brought Harold Godwinson to William bound in chains.

"Hail, Harold Godwinson," spoke William. "I have secured your release as an ally of Normandy. Your King Edward has named me his successor. Your assistance in England will be important to my reign. Swear now your allegiance and your freedom will be given you."

Harold was without alternatives. "I swear my allegiance to the rightful king of England," he vowed. William placed a ship at Harold's service and Harold returned to England. Among the ship's crew, William placed a spy.

Shortly after Harold's return, King Edward the Confessor expired. Harold Godwinson declared that Edward had named him his successor on his deathbed. He was immediately coronated in the newly-finished Westminster Cathedral. In Norway, Tostig had persuaded the warrior King Harald Hardraata to join him in invading the north of England. Hardraata was the most fearsome Viking warrior of all time. His campaigns had taken him all over the world, and everywhere he met with success.

On a strong northerly wind, Hardraata sailed with a large army to Scotland. The dwarfs were ready with the finest steel weapons to equip the Viking army. While Tostig travelled around the countryside raising his contingent, the ministers of Turold's court met with Hardraata. The dwarfs and the Vikings shared in a celebration. The battle axes the dwarfs had fashioned were the favored weapon of Hardraata's forces and the Vikings were eager to test them. For Hardraata himself, the dwarfs presented a fine battle sword and a chest full of gold.

Thus the Viking force was equipped and began the assault on England. Hardraata's standard was called *Land-Waster* and everywhere the Viking force was true to its name. Sailing south along the coast, they conquered town after town, taking booty in the Viking fashion. Tostig, Hardraata, and the finest dwarf-made weapons combined to form an awesome army of assault.

THE COMET

Turold stood on a hilltop in Normandy, watching the sky. A comet had appeared, growing nightly until it now lit up half the firmament. Through the balmy August night, Turold watched the comet sweep across the sky. It was frightening and beautiful to see the once familiar night-horizon ablaze with a new celestial body. Turold sensed a change in the world.

Bishop Odo had returned with a new sense of importance. He had secured the papal pennant for the invasion of England. William's forces would march under the standard of the church. William's spy returned from England with the news of Edward's death and Harold's hurried coronation. The Vikings, reported the spy, were plundering the coast and sailing south. Harold was preparing to march across England to surprise the Vikings at York in his first battle as the King of England.

Turold received the news of England calmly. He visited William to inform him that he would return to England at once.

"I shall sail to York to warn Tostig and the Vikings of Harold's approach," said Turold.

"No," insisted Bishop Odo, "let the heathens be surprised. We shall fight Harold who broke a Christian oath."

"I care not for your Christian skullduggery," said Turold. "Harold has the larger force and will no doubt prevail. I seek only to alert these allies and allow their escape."

"No," repeated Odo. "It is better if Harold defeats the heathens."

Turold remained silent in his resolve. Bishop Odo left abruptly.

On the Ouse river in Northern England, Hardraata and Tostig sailed together toward York, and at Fulford, en route to York, they met the combined forces of Earl Morcar and Earl Waltheof. A battle ensued and the Earls of York were defeated. Tostig and Hardraata took their warriors back to the ships to celebrate their victory and prepare for the plundering of York.

Turold was preparing to leave Normandy when a message came for him to meet Odo before he departed. So Turold and Odo met in private. The two were bitter enemies and Turold faced the bishop with suspicion. He carried his sword into the Bishop's chambers. Odo greeted him and brought out two glasses of wine.

"Let us drink to peace," said Odo. "There is surely some bargain whereby our differences might be resolved."

Turold raised his glass but refused to drink. He suspected the Bishop sought to poison him. Odo watched Turold carefully. He made light of Turold's refusal to drink the wine,

raising it to his own lips and drinking heartily.

"In Norman England we shall need to co-operate," said Odo. He described his plan for ruling England while he broke some bread and sliced a piece of cheese. Turold watched as Odo ate the bread and cheese, and only then did he slice a piece of cheese for himself.

"If Christians can learn tolerance, ours will be a peaceful land," said Turold. "We dwarfs have much we can teach you . . ." Suddenly Turold gagged; fighting for breath he looked at Odo in shock.

"Yes, Turold," Odo nodded, "I've poisoned you." Turold clawed at his throat. Odo held up the cheese knife.

"I smeared poison on one side of this knife. The first slice of cheese was untainted; the second was deadly. No more shall I be plagued by Turold's messages."

"One last message," Turold whispered, "waits for you in hell."

Turold the Messenger was dead and with him died the order that ruled the north before Christianity.

On the river Ouse, Tostig and Hardraata celebrated their victory. Hoping to avoid bloodshed, the people of York sent a message surrendering the town. The Vikings would meet the town leaders the next morning outside the gates of York. That night, Harold's army arrived after a forced march. They sealed the gates of York so that no word of their arrival could reach the ships.

The dawn brought a beautiful day to York. The sun was bright and a strong cool breeze blew the scattered clouds across the violet-blue sky, foretelling the approach of autumn. Tostig and Hardraata led half their men ashore in light mail, helmets, shields and short swords. Their battle axes and other fine dwarf arms they left aboard the ships. The men were jubilant;

they carried wine and food and joked about the cowardly fathers of York. As they approached the town all merriment ended. A cloud of dust hung over York, the dust raised by Harold's horses and infantry. Tostig, Hardraata and all the men ashore stood shield to shield in a Viking line. They fought long and bravely with their light weapons and they stood until every one of their number was slain. At Stamford bridge, King Harald Hardraata, the mightiest of Viking kings, died at the hands of the Saxons.

While the Saxons and the Vikings were engaged in battle, William and the Normans crossed the channel. They captured towns and supplies all along the south coast without resistance. They built fortresses and prepared for battle. When Harold returned from York, his army was tired and weakened. At Hastings, the forces met and the Normans prevailed. Harold Godwinson was slain and William was called the Conqueror, King of England.

Bishop Odo fought in the battle of Hastings. He and his clergy became the rulers of England. They administered the land, levied the taxes and kept the records. Under their rule, all heathens were banished. And so the messages of Turold brought about the rise of Norman England and the fall of the Kingdom of Aegol.

The Demise of Aegol

Witches and Dwarfs

The herb women and healers branded by the Christians as witches traded regularly with the dwarfs who had been similarly denounced. The heathen outcasts relied on mutual cooperation in the face of their persecution and hence the Christians pointed to a diabolical conspiracy calling the dwarfs the consorts of witches.

Hall of the Dead

In the last dark days of Aegol, the spreading plague claimed the lives of all who remained in the underground kingdom. The heirs of Prince Jord and Princess Hinne were carried to the Hall of the Dead in Aegol's last solemn ceremony. They were laid to rest amid the awful remains of their subjects and their kingdom. They carried with them to the grave the secret of Aegol's royal treasure, a fabled store of riches whose whereabouts remain unknown.

The Demise of Aegol

"Under Odo's leadership the Norman clergy spread the word of Christianity and outlawed heathen practices. The art and icons of the early days were destroyed. Makers of herbal medicines were persecuted as witches. The clergy instructed the people that dwarfs were in league with the devil. They outlawed the trade of food, clothing and essentials to dwarfs. Dwarfs were stoned and persecuted in villages where they once traded. The dwarfs of Aegol retreated into the underground Kingdom.

"Under this persecution, the newly elected Prince and Princess, Jord and Hinne, struggled to save their race. For many years they sought ways to adjust; dwarf traders met with village folk in secret and these clandestine traders demanded exorbitant prices for the most meager goods. The oppression was overwhelming. Dwarfs resorted to stealing food and chaos reigned in the Kingdom of Aegol. At last, Prince Jord and Princess Hinne decided on an evacuation.

"Many of the dwarfs cooperated in the building of ships and helped make arrangements. Others fled the Kingdom on their own. In the midst of this confusion, the Kingdom crumbled. The untended water supplies went stagnant. Filth and decay overtook the dwellings and the halls. Scraps of contaminated food were fought over. Before the evacuation could begin, disease broke out. In the underground confinement, the plague spread quickly. Prince Jord and Princess Hinne set a noble example, tending the sick and burying the dead. Soon an entire mine chamber had to be used as a mass grave. The Prince and Princess succumbed to the disease and were buried in the last solemn ceremony of Aegol. No new prince was elected.

"The Kingdom of the Dwarfs had fallen. The poet of these chronicles had carved the words 'Kingdom of the Dwarfs' above the stone doors of Aegol's entrance lest the place be lost forever. The doors were sealed then and covered with earth. All other entrances were blocked and the Kingdom's few survivors escaped by sea.

"Gentle reader, be you Christian or heathen, dwarf or man, heed these remembrances of greatness. Aegol is dead; let not its memory pass forever from earth."

Afterword

In March of 1980, all artifacts were returned
to the dig. The stone doors of the Kingdom
of Aegol were levered shut and the earth was
replaced in time for Sir Rupert Grootes to
replant his geraniums. The research party left
the site with the notable exception of Dr. Egil
Dvaergen.

Dr. Dvaergen disappeared on March 4th,
1980. A note he left asked us to bid farewell on
his behalf to Sir Rupert and the members of
the Royal Academy who came to witness the
closing of the dig.

It is the suspicion of the members of his team
that Dr. Dvaergen stayed inside the dig. At the
date of publication, his whereabouts remain
unknown.

September 31, 1980